Defiance Is Different
A Helen and Frank Story
Thomas Morgan

TMH Publishing

First edition

Cover Design: Jodi Parrish

ISBN (Print) 978-1-7376747-6-4
ISBN (ePub) 978-1-7376747-7-1

Also by

Thomas Morgan

The Helen and Frank stories

Available online as an eBook and Print On Demand
from Amazon, Barnes and Noble, Goodreads, Smashwords,
books2read, and many other sites.

#1

***Helen and Frank: Getting Older and Finding Love With
Food, Wine, Theater, Music,
Crime and COVID***

#2

***Marinated Money: Love, Crime and Capers in the Time
of COVID-19***

#3

Russians and Rubles

Please allow me to introduce myself. I'm a man
of wealth and taste. – *Sympathy for the Devil*
                    - Mick Jagger and Keith Richards

Don't feel unique to chaos. That's all we know
around here.
                            - A Catholic priest in St. Louis

Introduction

G rowing old is risky. Combine it with poverty and you have a conundrum. In *Defiance Is Different*, the fourth in the *Helen and Frank* series, Frank Palermo had lost his money by 2023. He had sent it to aid the defense of Ukraine, along with prodigious sums of money he had defrauded from Russian oligarchs. Helen Palermo was living on a placid lake in Florida, estranged from Frank, whom she feared might get her killed. Barney Browning and Vinnie Palermo continued to make money. They needed to invest it somewhere, so they began buying regional banks in the Midwest. Their success attracted unwanted attention. With Barney's help, Frank returned to his gastronomic roots and opened a small restaurant in Defiance, Missouri. Helen arrived from Florida and helped Frank's restaurant succeed. The Covid-19 pandemic was over, yet people had much to fear--multiple wars, urban crime, a porous southern border, inflation, ubiquitous fentanyl, inept and scary politicians, overreaching bureaucrats, a divided electorate, and a presidential election year. If 2023 was calamitous, imagine what 2024 might bring.

Chapter 1

Along the Missouri River near St. Louis, the villages of Defiance and St. Albans are separated by about two miles. Despite their proximity, the little settlements are remarkably different. St. Albans is a recently planned community with single-family homes and villas, an elegant country club, a comfortable inn, a manmade lake, and a historic general store, all of it enjoyed by wealthy residents and their visitors. Defiance down the river is older and faded ... some would say hardscrabble, dating back over 300 years to the early French and Spanish explorers. Before the arrival of Europeans, Native Americans had lived in the area for thousands of years, drawn by abundant game and fresh water.

After receiving a large Spanish land grant, Daniel Boone and his son, Nathan, built a home near Defiance over two hundred years ago. When Daniel Boone moved somewhere, American settlers followed, especially since Boone offered land for sale. The lure of dirt-cheap property west of the Mississippi River created a small land rush. Nobody thought to inform the Native Americans.

The area around Defiance today is characterized by wooded hills with older farmhouses and square patches of farmland. Defiance lies at the beginning of the historic Missouri River wine country originally settled by German immigrants in the early 19th Century. The unassuming hamlet sits around a curve in Missouri Route 94, a road that carries heavy traffic from St. Louis headed for the wineries. Defiance features a roadside bar and grill, a church, a plant nursery, a craft brewery, and a few nondescript buildings. St. Albans is open and inviting to the arriving visitor. Defiance is more secretive, largely hidden by its hilly wooded terrain.

Barney Browning purchased 100 acres of blufftop land with a river view east of Defiance in 2022 after the residents of St. Albans grew tired of Helen and Frank Palermo. Barney's property featured a small farmhouse with a winterized habitable barn and some resident goats. Barney hired a crew to modernize the house into a comfortable home for his growing family. His acreage stretched down the bluff to a dilapidated bar on Route 94 known as the Relay. This building had originally been a French restaurant called *Cafe Relais*, but few travelers chose to stop there. More economical places to eat and drink beckoned from the wine county a few miles down the road. After the Relais failed early in the Covid-19 pandemic, the genteel property had cycled through several owners until it devolved into a seedy biker bar everyone called the Relay.

Barney and his pregnant wife, Moselle, had taken a hotel suite near a suburban St. Louis hospital as her due date neared. After Frank Palermo left for Florida to find Helen, Barney spent his days cleaning up the house and barn in Defiance and installing a rudimentary security perimeter. Frank texted him on January 13 that he was returning to St. Louis in two days and asked for a ride. Barney met him at terminal 2, a congested arrival area with little parking. Frank scrambled into the armored Navigator while it was briefly stopped in traffic.

Barney gave Frank a fist bump. "Good to see you, buddy. Welcome home. How was Florida?"

"Warm and inviting as usual this time of year. Wish I could say the same thing about Helen. How's Moselle?"

"She's swollen, cranky, and ready to drop that baby. You were down there several weeks. Something must have gone right with Helen."

"She wanted a warm body at night and some conversation during the day. That's about all I can say. She dropped hints that I should go home after she got enough of that."

"Is she coming back?"

"Don't know … said she'd think about it. What's happening around here?"

"We're totally out of St. Albans. I've moved what's left of our operation over to Defiance. It's a whole different world over there. The house on the property is being renovated. The barn is habitable. I've got some security set up."

"I need to get a job. I'm broke."

"You've got the rental income from the St. Albans complex. You can live on that."

"Afraid not. I took a second mortgage on the St. Albans place to keep the battery caper going. Any income from the rental goes to service that extra debt."

"Well, Frank, my brother, it looks to me like you're scraping the bottom of the financial barrel. Lucky for you, you've inherited some money."

"What're you talking about?"

"Our friend, Mrs. Jenkins, over at Beaumont, you remember her from your wedding. Well, she passed on to her heavenly reward while you were in Florida. I opened a letter to you from her executor last week because I didn't know when you were coming back. It said she left Helen nine hundred grand ... you, one hundred."

Frank ignored the fact that Barney was opening his mail. "That old biddy, a millionaire? I can't believe it. She was as tight as two coats of paint. She didn't even like me."

"She liked you to the tune of one hundred large. She also left a million to Beaumont and two million to the Alzheimer's Association. She didn't acknowledge any family heirs in her will."

"Mrs. Jenkins, the multimillionaire … wonders never cease. I never even knew her first name. She was always Mrs. Jenkins to me. When do I see the money?"

"Not for a while. The letter said you should expect a check in a few months. We're talking about lawyers here, so I wouldn't hold my breath. Her full name was Thelma Ann Jenkins. She had her good and bad days at Beaumont. I liked her on the good days. She apparently outlived or disowned all her heirs."

"What am I supposed to do until then? I need a job."

"That's easy … I want you to run my investments. You're good at that … way better than the outfit I'm paying now. They speak a language I don't understand—all about options and derivatives. They're all talk and no production. You always made it simple. I've been copying your investments since before Covid. You made me rich."

"No way I can do that. That would be a violation of my consent order. If the feds find out I'm back in the investment business in any way, they'll come down on me like a load of bricks."

Barney scratched his chin. "Well, buddy, here's another possibility. When I bought the property in Defiance, it turns out I also bought a dive bar down the slope on Route 94. You can run it if you want to. That joint needs all the help it can get. I think you could turn it into something."

"I'm too old to run a bar. I don't think I have the energy … the stamina. You know what I mean?"

"Obviously, we'd get you some help. You'd just be the supervisor. I think they call that the executive chef nowadays. What about Andrea Simonetti ... that private chef you used before things went south in St. Albans? She'd be perfect in the kitchen with your know-how. You'd also need a bartender, somebody to wait tables, a bouncer or two. It's not a big place. I have some people in mind if you're interested."

"Barney, give me a break. I feel like I'm getting sandbagged here ... why would I need two bouncers?"

"I'm just thinking out loud. I'll take you by there, and you can have a look ... see what you think."

∾

Frank slept in a bedroom in the barn. Two of Barney's security people already occupied the other bedroom. Two others slept in bedrooms in the house while it was being renovated. Ten goats and two Great Pyrenees also slept in the barn, which gave the building a distinctive odor. The goats and dogs roamed Barney's property during the day, where the goats kept the weeds and grass under control. The dogs seemed annoyed with Frank, but the goats were friendly.

After familiarizing Frank with the new blufftop property, Barney took him down to the Relay on his second morning home. The annual January thaw had set in. Most of the snow was gone, replaced by puddles of water in the gravel parking lot. Barney let Frank out at the door and pulled the

Navigator around to the side lot. Without waiting for Barney, Frank, resplendent in khaki slacks, loafers and a windbreaker, walked past two large Harley motorcycles and entered the bar. The hazy interior smelled of sweat, tobacco, beer and marijuana. Two couples, all with multiple tattoos, sat at a small table around two large pitchers of beer. The bartender disappeared into the back room as soon as Frank entered.

"What're you doing in here, Grandpa?" The larger man said. "You need to head to one of them wineries down the road. That's where you look like you belong." The other three drinkers laughed.

"I'm Frank Palermo. I'm looking at a job here."

They all four laughed. The taller woman, in dirty jeans, a sweat-stained leather halter top, and blond, stringy hair, stood and said, "There ain't no job for you in here. You're too old to work. Hell, you look too old to be on social security. You're probably dead, and you don't know it yet. Now get out of here before we get mad. Then we'll have to throw your ass out."

Frank took a tentative step back. The two men, in faded jeans and leather vests, immediately stood and moved toward him. Frank braced himself to be bum-rushed out of the bar. Then Barney stood in the doorway.

Barney Browning, at 300 pounds and six feet 8 inches, cut off the faint January sunlight. The two men stopped and crouched into martial arts positions. Barney smiled and walked towards them. One of them screamed and launched a kick at Barney's chest. Barney stepped aside and gripped the errant foot at full extension with his right hand. He rotated the foot until an ankle ligament made a popping sound. The assailant fell to the floor, writhing in pain. "You son of a bitch! You broke by foot."

"It's just a bad sprain," Barney said. "I wouldn't break anything unless I really wanted to."

The second man, now a reluctant assailant, turned back towards the table. Barney kicked him squarely in the buttocks to send him flying across the table, splashing copious amounts of beer over the two women, who jumped up and cursed Barney. He grasped the writhing man with one hand and the flying man with the other and dragged them through the front door, depositing them in a large puddle of melted snow.

The larger man sat up and pulled a rusty nine-millimeter handgun from his belt. Barney kicked the gun across the parking lot. The would-be shooter screamed and then began whimpering.

Barney turned back to the women. "This place is under new management. We'll be closed for a few weeks to clean it up. After that, don't come back until you're sure you can behave yourselves. Get your stuff and get out." He pointed to the taller woman, "I hope you can drive that hog out there. Your old man is in no condition to use his foot right now. Put some ice on it when you get home, wherever that is."

Barney stood at the door to see them off while Frank held back. The four motorcyclists, shouting and making obscene gestures, mounted their bikes and rumbled away. It appeared that the taller woman could drive a hog.

"Are you sure two bouncers will be enough?" Frank said.

"Two of my men will be quite sufficient. Actually, one will do it. We need to change the ethos in this place. I can see that now. I'm sorry it had to get started this way. I should have come down here by myself and run off this trash. Now, you probably won't take the job."

"You're certainly right about one thing. Defiance is not St. Albans."

"Frank, please just think about it. I feel like we can make this place work for both of us. I hope you'll give this deal a chance."

"Barney, it's not like I've got a bunch of job offers right now. Let's look around this dump. I want to see the back room. I assume that's the kitchen. I've already seen enough of the barroom."

The kitchen was as dirty as the barroom but featured different filth. Thick layers of dirt, grease, and spilled food coated every surface. Dirty pots and pans were stacked in the double sink. Garbage spilled out of a large can—all of it contributing to a general smell of decay.

The bartender came out from behind a walk-in cooler. "Good morning, good sirs. Welcome to the Relay. What would you like to drink? Can I cook you some food? Maybe you would like some breakfast?"

"What's your name?" Barney said.

"Miguel Arena Cortez, at your service."

"Do you have a resume?" Frank said. "And you can drop the accent. I can tell you're not Hispanic."

"Yes, I have a resume. I don't keep it here."

"We're shutting down for a while to clean this place up," Frank said. "You can work on the cleanup crew at minimum wage if you want. Submit your resume if you decide to apply for a job when we reopen. We'll be putting more emphasis on food, less on booze."

In contrast to the Relay's first floor, the second floor was relatively clean and undisturbed. It featured three bedrooms and two full baths. Frank and Barney were surprised at its pristine condition and marveled that it had not served as a crash pad or worse for the biker crowd. The decent condition of the second floor was explained when it became evident that the bartender had been living in one of the bedrooms.

Barney provided a generous budget to transform the place. Frank immediately moved into an upstairs bedroom while the downstairs was being cleaned and remodeled. Living in the barn on the bluff was too odiferous for him, although he continued to walk up there on most days to visit the goats. He hired a crew from St. Louis County to clean the kitchen and bar. Then he had another crew tear out the drywall, pull up the floor, remove the suspended ceiling, and steam clean the exposed studs before installing new drywall. Removing the plastic floor tiles revealed old hardwood from the original construction. Ripping out the suspended ceiling exposed the original coffered ceiling. The original floor and ceiling were elegant and only needed cleaning.

He moved the partition between the barroom and kitchen to obtain more dining space. He shortened the bar and added four more tables for dining. He installed an updated commercial kitchen and a service window from the kitchen to one side of the shortened bar. As the interior work proceeded, he had the front and north sides paved for more parking space and cut a drive-through window for easy food pickup on the north side. Lastly, he installed a commercial smoker behind the building and a large patio with a sound stage on the south side. Covering the sound stage with a retractable awning allowed for a three-season outdoor music venue. He thought about renaming his place La Strada but decided against that plan. That name was too common. He kept the name Relay and prayed he would attract an improved clientele on the basis of better service and food.

Frank hired Andrea Simonetti to run the kitchen and she brought enough staff to launch the new operation. She gave him a four-month handshake commitment, telling him that after four months, the wedding season would require her full attention. Their new menu featured the usual roadhouse fare but added a few Italian dishes that Frank favored, including that St. Louis mainstay, toasted ravioli. The bar had a small display of liquor and a selection of local bottled beers but nothing on tap and no pitchers. Frank had never liked pitchers of beer. Consumption of beer in large quantities at his old restaurant too often led to sloppy behavior. He would add that feature only on sufficient customer demand. He did offer a few red and white wines by the glass and bottle, including a well-known Missouri Norton, a delightful dry red wine. The final touch of paint, varnish and polishing was completed by February 15, under budget and on time.

Barney dropped by the next day and was properly amazed at the Relay's transformation. "Sorry I haven't been around, Frank. I've been busy with Moselle and little Barnabas. That new baby is a full-time job." He looked around the dining area. "This is really nice. I can't believe I'm looking at the same place."

"It looks different because only the bones of the place are the same. Everything else has changed. Now, let's keep our fingers crossed that people will show up."

"It's incredible, Frank. Our house is about ready. I'll be moving the family in next week. I can't wait to see what you can make of this place."

"Prepare to be more surprised when you see what it cost you to do all this."

"Copying your investments made me rich, man. Let's spend some of it."

Frank did a soft opening on Friday, February 17. The weather was too cold for most bikers, but a few curious local couples and families stopped in over the first weekend to allow the staff to work out the bugs in their operation. Two local women from the church brought him an apple pie and a German chocolate cake as welcoming gifts, causing him to upgrade his opinion of the denizens of Defiance. He put a notice on social media on February 20 that the new and improved Relay was open. He did not bother with print, radio, or television advertising.

He had texted and left phone messages with Helen nearly every day since he returned from Florida, but she did not reply.

Chapter 2

The war in Ukraine continued in 2023. Inflation, street crime, and fentanyl deaths haunted the United States. The porous southern border was joined by a porous northern border with Canada. A replay of the chaotic year 2022 seemed in the making. As winter proceeded, cases of Covid-19 did not spike as widely feared, but people continued to argue about this welcome news as they had earlier argued about every other aspect of the disease. The FBI and Energy Department announced that the virus had likely 'leaked' from the Wuhan Institute of Virology. Federal health authorities also began to credit natural immunity as protection against the virus—acting as if this knowledge had always been obvious to them.

To Valentin Kostakovich Constantin, living in Road Town, British Virgin Islands, none of this mattered. Distance and wealth insulated him from these little worries. He had fled there with his girlfriend and a few associates when his banking business collapsed under the weight of theft and scandal. Val missed his life in New York City—the restaurants, bars, and adult entertainment, all within a short drive in his armored limousine. In Val's opinion, Road Town was misnamed. Road, in this instance, referred to the entrance to the harbor, not to any abundance of streets.

His girlfriend, Natasha Dimslie, had decamped for New York City after a month in Road Town, walking out of his life on New Year's Eve in a drunken rage. He had been so busy with his investments at Sunshine Bank that he had forgotten their dinner date. She made her dissatisfaction clear that evening by taking his antique revolver with her on the ferry to St. Croix. Val heard that someone had seen her throw it into the sea during the short voyage. It was her final gesture of contempt for him. Val missed his gun, a valuable 1895 Nagant, more than he missed Natasha. He knew a girlfriend would be easier to replace than the gun. A new girlfriend would also allow him to throw out his platform shoes. Natasha had been too tall.

Val loathed Road Town, but he had fewer options than Natasha. He was wanted by U.S. authorities and in trouble with the Kremlin. He knew he annoyed the criminal element that owned Sunshine Investment Bank in Road Town. They welcomed his wealth but not his physical presence in Road Town because he attracted unwanted attention from governments and law enforcement.

Although Val felt incarcerated, he went through the motions of being free. His major concern was his dwindling wealth. Natasha's exit left him with only two assistants—one for finance and one for other activities. He met with his finance assistant two days a week to go over his accounts. "What's happening with the hard carbon?" he asked, smiling at Monica Harris. Val wondered why he had never felt attracted to her.

"That asset has been sold and converted to South African Krugerrands," she said. "Your profits are in a bank in Madagascar."

"Madagascar. That's a very distant place. It seems I'm being pushed farther away from the center of everything." Val paused and prepared to ask a rhetorical question. "Please update me on our relations with First Baltic Bank."

"We are essentially cut off from that bank ... as we are with other outside financial conduits. Sunshine Bank here handles your money as they please. You are still blocked from withdrawing any assets from your accounts."

"So, my assets in Madagascar are my only real liquidity. Is that correct?"

"I'm afraid that is essentially correct, Mr. Constantin, not counting any assets you may have here in the house."

"Thank you, Monica. That will be all for now. Now, I'd like to confer with Alexis, and please have him bring me a cup of tea."

Alexis Smirnov was Val's fixer. He arranged everything from security to dinner reservations. "Good morning, Alex. What can you tell me about our friends, the Palermo clan?"

"The St. Louis contingent is continuing to consolidate their operation in a little town in Missouri known as Defiance. It looks like Frank Palermo is opening a restaurant outside of that town. Barney Browning, Frank Palermo's former bodyguard, seems to be running their operation now. He appears to have grown quite wealthy. We are trying to trace the source of his financial success. Vinnie Palermo, head of the Chicago contingent, has moved his center of operations to Lake Geneva, Wisconsin. He bought a large home on the lake there. He's a new father, and he's working from home. Vinnie continues to be successful in his business dealings."

"Thank you, Alexi. That was very concise ... exactly the way I like it. What about the woman, Helen Palermo?"

"She has been more difficult to trace. She and Frank Palermo seem to be estranged. We do have some new information that puts her on a lake in north Florida ... near a small town known as Interlachen."

"Good. That makes her the most isolated one of their despicable lot ... the most vulnerable. Am I correct?"

"That appears to be the case at this point. She doesn't have an obvious security detail. Please remember she is probably heavily armed. We understand she is a very competent marksman."

"Markswoman in her case … I've heard that too, but I've not seen much evidence to support her reputation. I do think she is the mastermind who dreamed up the battery scam they perpetrated on us. She has made my life miserable. Let's get our Wagner colleagues to pay her a visit. Can you arrange that?"

"I'm afraid not, sir. They say they are very busy in Africa. They also claim we didn't pay them in full for their last assignment."

"That's because they botched their last assignment. I paid them what they were worth. What can you arrange for us around here?"

"We can bring in some people from Haiti. I'm certain they won't be as skilled as the Wagner operatives, and they will insist on advance payment."

"Make it happen. I still have some cash here in the house. It will be the usual arrangement. They will get twenty-five percent upfront … the balance upon completion of the assignment. And be certain they aren't high on cannabis. I want them drug tested."

Alexis nodded assent and backed out of the home office. Val stood at the bay window that looked out over the harbor. Small sailboats dotted the azure water, some at anchor and others leisurely making their way out to the road and then to sea. The harbor seemed lonely to Val. The larger sail and power boats had emptied the quay—carrying rich people back to the States after the winter season in Road Town. The last of the cruise ships had departed as the summer heat approached.

Val knew he was a prisoner in a small tropical paradise. He needed to find a way to get to Africa, where he had wealth and connections.

☙

Vito Ragusa and Pasquale Salerno also met twice weekly—Vito in New York City and Patsy in Hallandale Beach, Florida. The video conference was recorded for further encryption and distribution to other interested parties in the organization. Vito and Patsy had hired the best electronic talent to make their conferences secure. With the final program, they felt satisfied that no prying minds could penetrate their electronic firewall. What they hadn't considered was that Rachel Bruggemann Palermo had made no effort to hack them because she was a busy new mother.

Vito took the lead as numbers filled the screen. "Here are our weeklies for the five boroughs. You can see our numbers are down across all our street operations except opiates, particularly fentanyl. That's one area the state hasn't taken over yet."

The screen next showed numbers from South Florida. "It's the same here," Patsy said. "Everything's down except fentanyl and methamphetamine. That's what keeps our street operation going. What about your warehousing and distribution activity?"

"It's pretty flat. We aren't growing much there because only a few people are going back to the office. That's what I'm thinking anyway. What about your waste management operation in Chicago. How's that doing?"

"It's showing a small uptick. People are going back to their offices in Chicago and making more garbage. That's one thing that works for us. We are also making money piping methane out of the landfills and recycling plastic. You'd be surprised how much gas those landfills produce."

"What about your pal, Vinnie Palermo? How's he doing?"

"He's not my pal, Patsy. We don't keep up with him much anymore. I'll check him out and let you know."

"Well, I've been following him, and I can save you some time. Vinnie's been busy. His warehousing and distribution software has become very popular. He's selling licenses to it all over the country. He's also back to building new commercial offices, and he bought a bank."

"Bought a bank? What's he want with a bank?"

He and that big guy Barney Browning ... he's Frank Palermo's muscle ... bought a regional bank in South Dakota. Vinnie seems to be using it to help finance his new construction around the Midwest. Vinnie seems to think commercial real estate is about to turn around."

"You're so smart, you should figure out what he's doing with the new construction. My sources hear he's building new apartments and hotels. He can make the change to office buildings when the time is right.

"How do you know so much about Vinnie?" Vito seemed puzzled.

"We follow him because whatever he's doing seems to involve us at some point. I don't want to get blind-sided by that Palermo crowd again."

"How does that Browning guy figure in the bank deal?"

"He's got a lot of money. I don't know where it's coming from. We think he's running his own scam. We just can't figure out what it is."

Vito distrusted Vinnie and Frank Palermo. He feared Helen Palermo, Frank's gun moll. Now, he also had to worry about Barney Browning. "We'll have to keep an eye on that bunch," he said. "The last time they got into banking, they cost us some serious money ... screwed our deal with First Baltic. What's new with our Russian friend in Road Town?"

"He's even more restless than usual ... won't stop bothering us about what he calls *his* money. We show him the numbers ... how well we're handling his investments. He keeps coming back the next day, asking the same questions. Our banking people in Road Town are sick of talking to him."

"Maybe he should cool off ... ah, take a long swim or something like that. You know what I mean?"

"Not yet. We're pretty sure he's got valuable assets hidden away in the house we're renting him. We need to get our hands on that before he has a change of lifestyle. You hear what I'm saying?"

∽

Margaret Benson's star had risen in the United States Treasury Department since she received credit for breaking up the Constantin brothers' money laundering operation. As the new deputy director of the investigations division, she supervised three assistant deputy directors and two secretaries. One assistant, D. Oliver Reginald Kraken, III, PhD., MBA, particularly interested her. He was arrogant, aggressive, reasonably informed, and moderately intelligent—all qualities that made him useful. The only alarming thing was she was certain he wanted her job. No one knew how Kraken got the job in Treasury. He was said to be independently wealthy. Margaret surmised he had an unknown patron in the current administration.

Margaret persisted in calling him Reggie—a familiarity she knew he hated. Kraken preferred to be addressed as doctor or professor. He had once held a faculty position at a private college in Ohio, but he had been let go when he failed to achieve tenure ... in addition to being a general nuisance. Upon arriving at Treasury, Kraken made certain everyone understood his government job was a temporary position for him. All his colleagues at Treasury agreed with this notion. Margaret knew that Reggie would never advance in government. His patronizing demeanor had alienated every government bureaucrat he encountered. She had her secretary call him into her office.

"Good morning, Reggie. I hope you had a pleasant weekend. I have a new assignment for you. Please have a seat."

Kraken had already moved to the chair before she offered it. Even when seated, he managed to keep his nose upturned as if he smelled a foul odor.

"I've opened a new Palermo banking file," she said. "I assume you are familiar with the original."

"Yes, I've read it." Kraken had, in fact, memorized the file. He suspected it had been heavily edited by Margaret to protect her failings in the original investigation.

"We brought down the bank in Cyprus that Frank Palermo was using to launder Russian oligarch money. Now the Palermo family and their associates have bought a domestic bank, Farm and Home Trust in Sioux City or somewhere out there."

"I read the file, Margaret. I know you're trying to extradite Valentin Constantin. I'm not sure there is anything left to do with that case until we can get our hands on Constantin. Frank Palermo is a has-been. We've closed him down completely."

"That's my point. Frank Palermo is history ... he's in the archives, but his nephew in Chicago is still a force, and Frank's bodyguard seems to have large, unexpected financial resources. They bought this regional bank. I want you to go out there and talk to the nephew and Browning ... I think he's their bodyguard. Find out what they're doing with their new bank."

"Isn't that a job for the FDIC? Why are we getting involved at this point?" Kraken sensed he might be walking into a bureaucratic trap.

"I'm sure you are aware that domestic banks are supervised by multiple federal agencies. This can lead to criticism of government oversight and accountability when something goes wrong in the banking system. We need to prevent that from happening. You can simply tell them we're interested in their activities because of past issues we've had with them."

"May I tell them you sent me?" Kraken studied Margaret carefully as he asked this question.

"Yes, of course, but they'll probably already know. I sense they keep up with us better than we do with them. These mid-sized regional banks are heavily leveraged with the run-up in interest rates. We need to get ahead of developments in that sector. We don't want any more bank failures."

Kraken returned to his workspace and opened the original Palermo file. He reviewed how Frank Palermo had used a bank in Cyprus to scam money from Russian oligarchs and funnel it to Ukraine. That part was widely known. He had to admit that using new battery technology as bait had been ingenious. The entire scheme had made the Palermo clan look like folk heroes—robbing from the evil rich and giving to the needy.

In the current Palermo operation, Barney Browning looked like a major player. That man needed further investigation. Kraken wondered again why the Palermo uncle and nephew had not been more vigorously prosecuted for violation of sanctions on Russian oligarchs. Granted, they had paid a large fine, but they both should have gone to jail. The reason for that lapse was unclear. It was almost as if they had some unknown leverage on Margaret Benson. An interview with those two might help him to understand and control his boss. Kraken liked control more than just about anything.

He asked one of their shared secretaries to arrange travel to Chicago and St. Louis. She told him she was busy with other assignments. The other secretary gave him the same excuse. The two women told him he would have to arrange his own travel. Kraken was not happy. He sent e-mails to Vinnie Palermo and Barney Browning announcing his intent to interview them. He then pasted the e-mails onto official Treasury Department stationery and mailed the letters to create a paper trail. He wanted them on his turf—at federal buildings in Chicago and St. Louis. His e-mails and letters stated that he expected Frank Palermo to be present at the St. Louis interview.

Chapter 3

Helen walked into the Relay early one afternoon in April. Frank was standing behind the bar drinking a San Pellegrino. The lunch crowd had departed, and the dinner crowd had not arrived. Frank tried and failed to hide his surprise. "Welcome to the Relay. What would you like to drink? I have to say I'm surprised to see you."

"It's good to see you too. Perhaps a glass of Chardonnay."

Frank had featured Chardonel and Norton wines by the glass at the Relay—two grapevines that could survive Missouri winters. He poured a glass of Chardonel and served it over the bar.

Helen stood behind one of the bar stools. She studied the wine and took a sip. "This is good, but it's not a Chardonnay. It tastes a little too metallic for me. We used to have Rombauer at our place in St. Albans. That's my favorite."

He took back the wine and pulled a bottle of Rombauer Chardonnay from the cooler—a bottle he had been saving for this very moment. "Something happened down there after I came back," he said. "Why don't we cut to the chase, and you tell me what happened."

Helen looked around the empty dining room. "You don't seem to be very busy. Let's sit down at a table, and I'll tell you about it."

Frank opened the Rombauer and brought two glasses to the table. They sat and stared at each other. Frank tried to smile but his facial muscles misbehaved. Helen smiled easily with her theatrical background. "I really like what you've done with this place," she said. "I've been following you on Facebook and Instagram. How's business?"

"Slow ... you were going to tell me what happened in Florida."

"There was a little altercation. I put in some outside security cameras and alarms. I didn't tell Teddy. One night, I saw two men with long guns up on the road around midnight. They walked around and then left. The next night, they came back and started to walk down the hill."

"What did you do?"

"I took out the M5 and put a few rounds into the hillside below them. They left in a hurry, and I've never seen them since that night."

"How did old Teddy take to that? By the way, Barney tells me they're calling that gun the M7 now."

"Whatever ... Teddy didn't mind. He keeps guns around, too. Remember that lake is out in the middle of nowhere. The neighbors around the lake were the ones who complained."

"Those people are mostly retirees living around that lake. I imagine you woke them up at midnight with your gunfire. Then they couldn't get back to sleep."

"They were unhappy ... and scared. They told Teddy they couldn't sleep at night. They kept after poor Teddy. They wouldn't talk to me. I was always the mystery woman down there. After that night, they never spoke to me again. So, I'm back."

"Back ... as in this building?"

Helen sighed. "That's where we're sitting. What kind of question is that?"

Frank remembered he had never bested Helen in a verbal joust. In the words of his hero, Yogi Berra, this conversation seemed like Deja Vu all over again. Frank tried to sound more intelligent. "I guess you also ran out of diversions down there."

"That wasn't it. Teddy was very good to me. He shopped for me when he went to town. We went over to St. Augustine a few times for dinner. That's a beautiful town, but it's getting very crowded. The weather was perfect—cool nights and warm days. I spent most of my time reading on the front lawn ... enjoying the view."

Frank had never thought of Helen as a contemplative type, particularly when there were snakes and alligators around. She had always been a doer. "Reading," he said.

I was studying more modern playwrights—Shepard and Albee are good. You know I like drama. I love Tracy Letts. Have you seen the movie August: Osage County?"

Frank had not heard of any of these people. Opera provided more than enough drama for him. "I'm sorry, I don't know much about literature. I'm trying to start a restaurant here. It's kept me very busy. I'm sure you know I'm broke."

"I know all that. I text with Moselle almost every day. I also frequently talk to Rachel. I follow you through them. I can help you with the restaurant. I'd be very good at chatting up the customers."

"Where are you staying?" Frank said.

Helen frowned. "I can stay anywhere I want to stay. I hope I can stay here."

"This place has three bedrooms and two baths upstairs. It's clean but small—nothing like what we had at St. Albans."

Darling, I know that. Barney told me all about this place. Do you have any security set up?"

Frank realized that Helen had been talking to everyone in their group except him. "Just the usual door and window alarms. I worry more about alcohol and cash walking out of here than somebody breaking in."

"Please forgive me, darling, but you really need to be more realistic. You've got organized crime here in the

States, and half the Russian oligarchs extremely unhappy with you—not to mention those two crazy banking brothers from Moldova. We're going to have to set up better security."

"Lucky for me, it's only half of the oligarchs. The other half of them have recently died."

"Unlucky for you, one individual in the surviving half is the biggest oligarch of them all ... and a thoroughly evil man. Did you know Barney and Vinny bought a bank?"

Helen had a talent for ending statements of fact with an unnerving question. Frank played for time. "I don't think I've heard about that. You know I've been very busy here. I'm sure you can tell me about it."

"They bought a regional bank in South Dakota or somewhere up there north of Omaha. I'm surprised you don't know about it."

"There you go again. I really don't know anything about what they're doing, and I don't want to know. I signed a consent order with the feds to stay out of financial matters. I'm trying to simplify my life ... keep out of trouble." Frank stopped himself from saying more. Helen could play the matador if she chose. He would not be the picador. A quieter life beckoned, but he remembered that complications always followed when Helen became involved in his affairs.

Helen flashed another theatrical smile and said, "You can lead any kind of life you like. I just got a big check from the Thelma Jenkins estate. I understand she left you a little money, too. We can use the money to simplify our lives together."

Frank thought his inheritance was more than a little, but he kept silent. He had been lonely and missed Helen. He feared her version of simplifying their lives would bring unusual changes, but he was ready to share the future with her.

After another glass of wine, he helped Helen move her things up to the second floor. She surveyed the bedrooms and chose the largest one with a king-size bed. "That bed looks like the one we had at St. Albans."

"It is. I moved it over from our place there. I sold most of the furniture to the new renters. Their restaurant in St. Louis is really doing well."

"I'll sleep on the left by the phone if you don't mind. That's the side I can adjust to a softer feel. Please hang my clothing in the closet. I'll unpack the suitcase myself ... and thank you for taking me back. I'll take this bathroom. You can have the one down the hall."

They slept together that night in the big bed—Frank with his CPAP machine and thick woolen socks and Helen wearing only her pink sleep mask, her handgun, and a bottle of zaleplon on the bedside table. It was an unusual conjugal bed, but it was the best they could do.

Helen immediately applied herself to remake the restaurant's operation. She hired two local influencers and a podcaster to advertise the Relay on social media. She visited the women's group at the local church and the staff at the plant nursery—handing out samples of food and talking up the Relay with anyone who would listen. She persuaded Andrea to add what Helen called 'road food' to the menu, mainly loaded nachos, hot wings and a larger selection of burgers. She added live music on Thursdays to the outdoor venue, expanding weekend entertainment to four days. She banished Mozart and Puccini from the sound system and played Shania Twain and George Strait tapes when live bands weren't playing. She circulated in the dining room and outdoor seating area from four p.m. to closing time. Helen was soon on a first-name basis with the growing number of regular customers.

As business increased, Frank wondered if their new success was from Helen's exertions or her reputation as an armed and dangerous woman. Cause and effect mattered little. The Relay was finally flourishing.

A few days after Helen began remaking the Relay, a clean-shaven young man with his long hair in a bun walked into the Relay. He approached Frank and said, "Good morning, Mr. Palermo, I'm Alan Ackerman, I saw your sign outside, and I'd like to apply for a job."

They shook hands. Frank studied the man. "I think I've seen you before, but I can't remember when."

"I was in here in January with some, ah ... former friends. We had a little dust-up with Mr. Browning. You may remember."

"Right ... now I remember. You look different."

"My life has changed. I've gotten off the dope and speed. I've stopped drinking. I'm in a Vivitrol program over in St. Louis County. It's turned my life around."

"I'm certainly happy to hear that, and I'm glad they're no longer your friends. You were running with the wrong people. Do you have a skill? What can you do?"

"I've been a short-order cook. I can wait tables and tend bar. I'll bus tables and wash dishes if that's what you need. I live around here, and I need a job."

"I certainly know that feeling, and I need all of those things. Get me your resume and three references. I'll look it over and get back to you."

"Resume?"

"Son, you *are* starting from scratch. Get me the names and phone numbers of people you've worked with. You can do that, right? Now come into the kitchen, and let me see you fry eggs and bacon."

❧

The long Memorial Day weekend passed in a blur of customers, food and music at the Relay. The restaurant had finally caught on with the locals. Visitors from the nearby wineries also began to eat and drink there. Frank's roadhouse was turning a profit. Andrea Simonetti and her crew had departed to cater for summer weddings--their peak earning season, but Alan Ackerman had become an acceptable cook under Frank and Andrea's tutelage. Frank was also able to hire and train several local women to work the dining area with

Helen's supervision. The business required more effort than either of them wished. Frank began to look for a manager.

Frank had closed the restaurant on the Tuesday following the hectic Memorial Day weekend for a private dinner for family and friends. Barney, Moselle, Vinnie, and Rachel joined Helen and Frank. The new Browning and Palermo babies, little Barney and Esther, were old enough for a babysitter up at the Browning house atop the bluff. Rachel's Australian shepherd, Cane, was also up there trying to herd the goats and make friends with the two Great Pyrenees. The goats now numbered fifteen.

The six of them gathered in the dining room in late afternoon over a meal of chicken spiedini, house-made gemelli with fresh herbs, grilled eggplant and a Greek salad. Frank served copious amounts of wine and beer, and Helen kissed everyone.

"Helen joins me in thanking you for coming. It's been a wild four months, but the restaurant is finally thriving. Helen's ideas have really helped us. I'm so busy now I'm starting to look for a full-time manager. Barney and Moselle get all the credit for financing this operation. We're now starting to pay them back."

"This spiedini is really good, dear uncle," Vinnie said. "I could almost believe your cook is Italian if I didn't know better."

"Alan is a quick study and a hard worker. Andrea had time to work with him before she left. He's really turned his life around since he got off all the bad stuff he was doing. He's also acquired better friends."

After a dessert of fresh strawberry pie and vanilla ice cream, Helen said, "I'd like to walk up to see the babies. We can talk freely on the way. The property has been swept free of surveillance devices. I have some speech-canceling software on my phone. We can talk freely just in case someone might try to listen in."

The big meal caused them to walk slowly. After some small talk about the progress of the new Browning and Palermo babies, Helen said, "I'm very curious to know how the new bank venture is going. Do either of you care to talk about it."

Barney took the lead. "We bought that regional bank in Sioux City to help finance new apartment and hotel construction in the upper Midwest. Vinnie is doing it modular, so we'll have the capability of converting everything to office space if that market ever comes back."

"The bank is strong ... a lot of rich farmers up there, and the energy market is still going strong in Montana and the Dakotas," Vinnie said. "What's changed in the last few months is many regional banks are stressed with the bank failures on both coasts and the run-up in interest rates. Many banks solicited too many brokerage deposits, and they bought long-term bonds. All these mistakes put them in a bind when interest rates shot up."

"That provided us the opportunity to buy several other regional banks at a big discount," Barney said. "We now control a system of regional banks from the Dakotas down to Texas."

"Very clever, gentlemen," Helen said. "You've got Midwestern agriculture and energy at your fingertips, top to bottom."

"Thanks, Helen," Barney said. "We're not only going for economy of scale. We're also trying to give superior service and more favorable loan and deposit rates. We're doing that by closing some branches and ramping up online banking. Most banks are making it harder for small businesses to borrow money these days. By closing some branches and offering robust online banking, we can lower our overhead and offer more favorable rates on our business loans."

Helen smiled. "You're impressive, Barney. Where did you learn so much about banking?"

"Both sides of our family go way back in banking. My grandfather started one of the first black-owned banks in southern Georgia. Moselle's father and grandfather were active in banking in southeast Kansas. In those days, they were groundbreakers in finance for people of color."

Frank tried his best to ignore this conversation, but his curiosity would not allow it. He could see a very lucrative opportunity in this banking foray. He could also foresee new scrutiny coming from federal regulators. "I'd be concerned you'll start to hear more from federal banking regulators about what you're doing."

"We already have," Barney said. "We've jumped through all the hoops with the feds and the states to get this thing going. Now, some turkey from Treasury is coming out here next week to talk to me. He says he's also going to Chicago to check out Vinnie. He wants to meet with you while he's in town."

"I should sit that one out. If I show up at the meeting, it'll look like I've gotten back into investments and finance. That would be a violation of my consent order."

"What do you want me to tell this guy?" Barney said.

"Just tell him the truth. That's the easiest thing to remember ... that I'm retired from finance, and I'm trying to run a small restaurant. Tell him I'm very busy. Bring him out to the Relay if he wants to see what I'm doing." Frank could not help adding, "Vinnie, I'm surprised your friends on the East Coast haven't gotten involved. They like money, and they remember Sutton's Law."

"Ditto on that," Vinnie said. "I've already heard from Patsy Salerno in Hallandale Beach. They want to invest in what we're doing. Apparently, Farm and Home Bank looks attractive to a lot of people ... and please stop calling them my friends."

"There goes the neighborhood," Helen said.

Chapter 4

Reggie Kraken made his way to St. Louis after several false starts, including canceled flights and difficulty procuring a meeting room in the Robert Young Federal Building in St. Louis for his interview. He finally met with Barney, Vinnie and their banking executives in early June. Vinnie had flown down to St. Louis to forestall Reggie going to Chicago, which would only complicate matters.

Reggie entered the meeting room an unhappy man. He was wearing a new N95 mask and carrying a large briefcase. He liked the inquisition style of meeting where he could sit at the end of a long table and skewer his adversaries with difficult questions. This encounter had already become flawed.

Where's Frank Palermo?" he said when they all were seated.

"You can take off the mask," Vinnie said. "The pandemic is over, and we can't understand what you're saying.

As for Frank, he's totally out of finance and investment. There's no reason for him to be here. He's running a restaurant out in Defiance. It's a full-time job."

"Defiance? I've never heard of it. I specifically said in my letters to you that I wanted him to be here."

It's a small town out on the Missouri River," Barney said, "About 40 miles west of here. We'll take you out there if you want to see it. I thought this meeting was about our banking activities ... not Frank Palermo."

Reggie tried to collect himself. "I didn't come out here to see some restaurant in the boondocks. I want you both to know that we've been watching your acquisitions. We're concerned at Treasury that your bank has become overleveraged. I want to see your books."

Barney, because of his physical bulk, could dominate a meeting no matter the seating arrangement. Sitting at a small conference table with Kraken and Vinnie, he loomed very large. "We've kept the FDIC and other relevant authorities abreast of what we're doing. I don't see where your department fits into this."

"We simply don't want to see another regional bank go under because of mismanagement ... that's all. The pandemic has made it more difficult for on-site monitoring."

Barney smiled, "The pandemic is over. Even the U.S. government and WHO are saying it's over. Nobody wants to hear about the pandemic."

That's why I'm here. We're going to do more on-site monitoring."

"If that's all you want, take a look at our books. It's all in this binder. Our bank has already passed the FDIC, the OCC, Federal Home Loan outfit, the regional Fed, and all the state regulators," Vinnie pushed a thick binder across the table. "If you can't get through the whole thing, there's a three-page exec summary in front."

Reggie tried to regain control of the interview, but cogency failed him. "I didn't come here to accuse you of anything beyond overreaching. I want you to know that we are watching you closely. As your bank grows, your need for capital reserves grows too." Kraken took a breath and waited for their response.

"So, you're watching us," Vinnie said as he and Barney rose and walked to the door. "Now you can watch us leave. If you have a specific issue with Farm and Home Bank, put it in writing. Meanwhile, we're going to a late lunch at the Relay. The grilled chicken spiedini with fresh herb pesto is very good there. You should try it. Frank Palermo will be glad to ship you some of the frozen stuff. The fresh version is much better."

❧

After dropping their bank executives off at FAHB headquarters in Chesterfield, west of St. Louis, Barney and Vinnie proceeded across the Missouri River to the Relay.

Helen and Moselle joined them around plates of Frank's newly famous chicken spiedini. Frank brought over a bottle of Chianti Classico. They were the only diners in mid-afternoon.

"Well, how did it go?" Frank said.

"You sure you wanna know? We told the treasury guy you're out of this stuff ... running a famous restaurant now."

"Please don't patronize me. Just give me the overview. I'm intrigued by this Kraken character."

"He strikes me as an inflated fool," Vinnie said.

"Remember, he's connected to Margaret Benson at Treasury," Frank said. "I think young Margaret still wants her pound of flesh from us. She's probably using Kraken as her foil."

"He didn't add anything to all the other regulators we've dealt with," Barney said. "We just need to watch out for the wrath of little Margaret. She's looking for a way to stick it to us if she thinks the bank's getting too big."

"Uncle Frank, would you send Kraken some of your frozen spiedini? I mentioned it to him."

In this peculiar way, conversation meandered from unexpected requests to strong opinions as the level of Chianti fell in the bottle. Helen and Moselle left to return to the blufftop house. The men moved to a table in the kitchen, and Frank opened another bottle of Chianti.

"We seem to be acquiring some more enemies," Barney said. "You feel safe living down here on the road, Frank? You really have no security down here. I worry about you two. You and Helen should be staying with us up on the bluff."

"I have Helen," Frank said.

The others waited, and Frank continued. "My friend in Florida, Teddy, told me the full story of her dust-up with the intruders down there at the lake that night. She didn't just shoot up the ground in front of them; she shot up their rental car up on the road."

"She must have had night vision capability with that little rifle," Barney said.

"Anyway, the Haitians nursed their car out to Highway 19, where it died. The local deputies picked them up. They had ditched their weapons, but the sheriff held them for false documents. Somebody paid a lot of money to get them extradited to Road Town, where they faced petty charges."

"That somebody would have to be Val Constantin," Vinnie said.

"Helen wore out her welcome down there with that stunt. Teddy says the folks around the lake are still talking about her ... that's why I say I have Helen."

"You don't want to get Aunt Helen excited when she has a gun in her hands. But I think Barney's right. You two should sleep up at the blufftop house. Security's a lot better up there."

❦

Val Constantin hated Road Town in summer. The tropical sun oppressed him, but he found the lack of entertainment even more oppressive. The tourists were largely gone, and the wealthy people who wintered there had departed for Maine and northern Michigan. One day in late June, as he sat idly in his office, surfing the internet, two men walked past his assistant and entered his office. Speaking English with a Russian accent, they identified themselves only as being from the FSB, Russia's current designation for its secret police. Val knew better than to ask for any identification. He motioned them to seats and waited.

"Mr. Constantin," One of them said. "We have come here to address your activities with First Baltic Bank in Moldova."

Val forced a smile and remained silent. He tried to stifle his fear and concentrate on what these two wanted.

"Mr. Constantin, we are interested in how almost two billion U.S. dollars passed through First Baltic Bank and into the hands of criminals in Ukraine."

"That's a question you should ask my brother, Vladimir. He was the principal of the Bank in Chisinau."

"Your use of a verb in the past tense is very interesting. Finding your brother has been a problem for us. It's why we are here. We have been unable to locate him."

"I think he might be in New York City."

"We have not found him to be living there at this time. In fact, we have found no evidence of his whereabouts living at any location."

Val listened closely. He could not discern how much these two men knew. They were clearly not Wagner, and they were a cut above low-level FSB agents. "I am not my brother's keeper."

"Mr. Constantin, we have evidence that you are your brother's keeper. You have been conducting financial transactions in his name here in Road Town. Is he hiding here? Are you concealing him?"

"I told you I don't know where he is."

"If you cannot produce him, we have to conclude that you have eliminated him."

"That's preposterous! I would never kill my brother."

"We have retrieved skeletal remains from the main furnace in your New York City condominium building. The DNA of those samples matches your brother's genetic profile. This is a fact."

Val tried to control his face. The FSB had resources that he hadn't considered. He began to feel the Kremlin's tenacles closing around him, and he knew his face gave him away. Val was an accomplished liar, but he was less proficient with nonverbal communication. "What do you want from me?"

"We want you to cooperate with us. We want to get back our stolen assets in Ukraine, and we want to punish the people who have stolen so much from us."

"How do you propose I do that?"

"First, please know that we have attached your resources in Mauritius. You'll get those assets back if you work with us. With that fact in mind, we want you to eliminate the Palermo family and their friends."

"I've tried that part. They are harder to kill than you might think. They're a very tough bunch."

"We are aware of that. We have some special talent that we can lend you. After you have accomplished that task, we will return your assets and arrange for you to fly to Africa."

I am grateful for the second part, and I will need your special talent to accomplish the first part."

"We will provide the talent."

With that, the two strangers walked out, leaving Val to consider why the Russians needed to find someone to kill the Palermo and Browning gang. Killing people was their specialty.

❧

Vito Ragusa of the New York families and Pasquale Salerno of the South Florida faction met in person at Vito's Long Island beachfront house in July. It was considered a modest house in the Hamptons, having only five bedrooms, but it had a magnificent view of Long Island Sound. They sat far out on the lawn, drinking Scotch.

"This is the life, don't ya think?" Vito said as he sipped his drink. "We're out of the crime-infested city, and our businesses are doing well."

"Every one of them? I don't think the Chicago operation is doing so hot."

"It's breaking even, Patsy. We just need to give it a little more time."

"The Palermo clan and this Browning guy are building a banking empire right under our noses out there."

"You're talking about Farm and Home Bank. It's growing, I can't deny that."

"That bank is right in the middle of the country. It's big but not too big. We really need a piece of it ... try to control it. It's the perfect match for our Road Town bank."

"That bank has been a tough nut to crack. The New York families have been buying their stock and bonds, but we can't get control of their holding company. They're pretty smart; they've issued two classes of stock. The class of stock they're selling us is crap."

"What about their bonds?"

"They haven't listed much in the way of bonds. They seemed to have a lot of money, and we can't buy our way into them."

"Well then, Vito, what we need to do is dirty their reputation. Maybe we could get a run going on their bank."

"How do we do that?"

"First, we use your *servitore* at Treasury to trash them quietly. Then we get it going on social media that they're in trouble ... very overextended. It's a shame how they mismanaged their bank."

Vito smiled at Patsy. "You got good ideas, Patsy. You're very with it on things like this. I'm impressed. I'll talk to our guy at Treasury. He can leak it to a couple of newspapers. We'll buy that bank out, one way or another."

"Don't worry about newspapers. Nobody reads those rags anymore. If it's in the papers, it's old news. Have your moron at Treasury leak it to some bloggers and influencers I know. I have a whole crew working on this. I'll have them send you the leads."

"Thanks, Patsy. This may be the way to go. We'll keep buying their stocks and bonds through our holding companies and LLCs."

"These days, it's all about our look, our narrative. We get our story out there, and the other guy looks bad. That's the way we do it now."

Patsy thought the New York families were wasting time and money trying to buy a bank outright or even control it indirectly. Their offshore bank in Road Town was doing well because it was lightly regulated. It had attracted a rich group of clients from throughout the world. A mainland bank was prey to a horde of regulators, most of whom didn't talk to each other. Dealing with the Palermo family and their friends added a further complication. He was certain about one thing: After his weekend with Vito on Long Island, the intellectual center of the East Coast organization had shifted from New York City to South Florida. In his mind, the change was appropriate. Many organizations and people were leaving New York and moving to Florida.

Chapter 5

Vinnie and Barney tried to count their enemies. They knew Val Constantin was after them, but he seemed to be quarantined in Road Town. The two hitmen he sent to kill Helen in Florida were laughable. Margaret Benson of the Treasury Department hated them, but the emissary she dispatched to harass them seemed hapless. The East Coast mob hovered around the edges of their businesses, but they had no leverage over Farm and Home Bank. They continued to license Vinnie's warehousing and distribution software, a package that was making them significant profits.

Wagner Group was a more dangerous animal altogether. July showcased their bizarre behavior, extreme even for Wagner. They pulled out of the war against Ukraine and staged a march on the Kremlin. This looked like a coup attempt, but was it? Prigozhin denied it, saying he only wanted to root out corruption and help Mr. Putin. Even stranger was their halting the march midway and moving to Belarus after announcing a deal with Putin. Once there, members of the group intimated they might have designs on neighboring Poland, further inflaming a sensitive border relationship. It was all very alarming: a paramilitary group of convicts who failed to defeat Ukraine, then marched on Moscow, now relocated to Belarus and trying to pick a fight with NATO.

One thing Vinnie and Barney knew for certain. Russian oligarchs had been relieved of billions of U.S. dollars by Frank's battery scam. Elements connected to the Kremlin were very unhappy about that swindle. They meant to get even. How they would do it remained unclear. Would it be the Wagner Group or some other villains dispatched by the Kremlin?

In their weekly telecom call, Barney said, "I think we can discount Constantin, at least for now. He's a virtual prisoner in Road Town. I just wish we could get inside his mind."

"Rachel's working on that."

"Rachel's back in business? Hot damn! That gives us an edge."

"She's just poking around. She turns out to be like an Italian grandmother when she thinks somebody is threatening her family. I'm also guessing motherhood isn't keeping her busy enough. Her network is picking up chatter between him and several Kremlin operatives. She's into his cell phone traffic and is working on his e-mail. We're trying to get a bug in the house he's renting down there. We're pretty sure the Kremlin is calling the shots with him now."

"Constantin is a known quantity. I can't figure out Wagner. I think they're likely to come after us. I'm just not sure whether they're still working with the Kremlin." Barney sat at his desk and munched on dried fruit, his current weight control regimen.

"Rachel thinks the whole march on Moscow thing was a ruse to get Prigozhin out of the war. His boys were getting chewed up. He did that crazy march on Moscow. Then he went to Belarus. Now we hear he died in a plane crash. I'm not sure he was even on that plane, and I have no idea why he was in Moscow in the first place ... if he was actually there. I guess Putin may have taken him out, but he still needs Wagner." Vinnie paused to think about what he was saying. "This is beginning to sound like a barroom conversation."

"There are many paramilitary groups in Russia besides Wagner," Barney said. "Putin can choose his villains from a cafeteria line. What about our Italian friends on the East Coast?"

"They seem to be of two minds. They want a piece of our income, especially our bank, but they're constrained by my licensing agreement, which is making them a ton of money. They don't want to lose that."

"They're not trying to strong-arm you?"

"Not yet." Vinnie smiled. "They really don't know what to do with me. I'm not one of them, but I'm Italian. And I'm making them a lot of money. I'm out, but I'm in ... if you get my drift."

"Trust me ... you're in, dude. They just haven't made it clear to you yet."

"I know they're still sore about us tanking their laundry deal with First Baltic in Moldova. But then Frank showed them another way to wash their money. So, they're of two minds about that beef, too." Vinnie signed, "I wish we could get Frank back into finance. He's a genius with money."

"He won't talk to me about money or investments."

"Aren't you getting enough of that through his restaurant? When I was down there, it looked like that was going really well."

"He's paid off my loan. All I'm getting now is rent for the building. And now he wants to buy the building. He and Helen are really minting money with the restaurant. She's got that place humming. Everybody that comes along Highway 94 seems to be stopping there."

"Aunt Helen is a genius with sales, and Uncle Frank is a genius with money. We need to get them both involved with the bank. By the way, you may not know this, but that crazy battery operation he set up in Bangalore is actually making money. They've started sending him a big chunk of money every month. Uncle Frank is on his way to getting rich again."

❧

Valentin Constantin had another visit from the two FSB men on the first of August. They entered his office at precisely 10 a.m., brushing past his assistant and taking seats across from his desk. "Mr. Constantin, we are happy to help you with the talent we promised you. We're giving you two solutions to your problem with the Palermo clan. These are simple solutions; we propose either an explosion or a toxin."

"Do you want to talk about this out on the pier?"

"Why? Are we being monitored in here?"

"I don't think so, but you can't be too careful these days."

"This is a simple plan. We have identified two people working in their restaurant as potential couriers. They're addicts ... how do you say it in America ... junkies."

"Now we say they have an opiate use disorder ... if it matters to you."

"No, it doesn't. Whatever you want to call it, we can feed them fentanyl and amphetamines, and they'll take a package for us into the restaurant in that little town."

"If it's a poison, how would you get the targets to drink it?"

"We've got a plan for that. They both drink bottled water. Your courier simply adds it to an opened bottle. When one of them drinks it, your problem is solved."

"I like the bomb idea better. *Your* courier simply takes it into the restaurant ... maybe down to the basement ... and you detonate it remotely. It can be made to look like a gas leak." Valentin noticed that one of the FSB men did all the talking. He looked directly at the silent man and said, "I have to tell you, I'm wondering why you don't do this yourselves. I'm sure your superiors would shower you with rewards."

"The answer is that it's difficult for us to get into America. We've been banned from entry."

Val knew they needed an intermediary—someone to give them plausible deniability if their plan went wrong. He also knew their proposal sounded like a suicide mission. Val pondered how he had descended from a high-flying New York City banker to a suicide bomber in rural Missouri. It was a thought best avoided. "How do you plan to get the package into their restaurant?"

"You pick up the package in downtown Chicago and connect with the couriers in St. Louis. They deliver the package."

"Why don't your couriers pick up the package themselves? What do I have to do with it? You're forgetting that I'm not welcome in the U.S. anymore, either. The federal authorities want to arrest me."

"The couriers won't go to Chicago ... they say it's too dangerous. Anyway, they're country people, not city people. You're the man who connects them with the package. We will fly you into Chicago. You don't have to go through their immigration process. You make the transfer, and we fly you out. After that you're free to fly to Africa. We guarantee it."

"Who guarantees it?"

"You have the assurance of my government and other parties that are working with us."

A guarantee from the Russian government offered Val little comfort. "I still don't understand why you need me. You're also forgetting I'm a virtual captive here. The Sunshine Bank people don't like me."

"Don't worry about them. We're all working together on this. Now, we need you to work with us."

"I still don't understand."

"What is there to understand? It's your needs we're talking about here. You need to get out of this little place where you live. It's like an exile for you. You need your wealth and power back. We're giving you that opportunity."

Valentin Kostakovich Constantin suspected he was being baited into a trap. He simply could not identify who was setting it. Was it the Kremlin, a Russian paramilitary group, the East Coast mob, or someone else? He decided to play along to find the answer. He also began to set a trap of his own. "Okay," he said. "I'll work with you on this, but I need some earnest money from you or whomever you represent. I want five million delivered to this account number at my bank in Mauritius. That's five million in U.S. dollars." He smiled as he handed them a business card with the pertinent information for his bank in Port Louis, Mauritius. "You do that for me, and I'll take care of the details of delivering the package for you."

Both men seemed surprised. "We'll have to get back to you on the earnest money question," the talkative one said. "We are not authorized to disperse such large sums. But I think an arrangement can be worked out."

❧

Alan Ackerman's cooking skills at the Relay became a sensation. His reputation spread rapidly by word-of-mouth and in social media—hallmarks of how St. Louis restaurants become successful. He was named a maestro of modern Italian and American cooking in a national food magazine, a recognition that Helen had arranged. Local food publications rushed to feature him and begged for his recipes. Travelers made special plans to dine at the restaurant. Locals became regulars, and wine-country visitors stopped in every day.

The Relay restaurant was doing so well that Frank felt unneeded. With Alan in the kitchen and Helen supervising the dining room, he began to take days off and concentrate on his cash flow and investments. He did this work alone without consulting his financial advisors, and he did his internet research on a secure and encrypted link. He knew that many people with malign interests were watching him for another financial misstep. Frank had never expected to grow rich again. He was determined to do it quietly this time.

Frank thought about promoting Alan to restaurant manager, but he knew that would upset Helen. If he tried to name Helen as manager, that would upset her too since she was a co-owner of the restaurant. He decided to abandon formal titles and accept reality. Success was its own argument. He called Alan to his tiny office one hot August mid-afternoon when business had slowed. "The Relay is really booming, and you're a big part of our success. We're doubling your salary. You are now our executive chef."

"Thank you, Mr. Palermo. I appreciate the opportunity you've given me here. I'm getting my finances in order, and my wife and I'm active in our church again." Alan paused and said, "If you don't mind, I'd like to talk to you about your new hires."

Frank waited. Alan seemed hesitant. "I don't know if you've noticed this, but the two women you just hired to work the outside tables are opiate users."

"*We* hired them, Alan. You interviewed them, too. I've noticed they sometimes seem sluggish."

"If you've been a user, you can spot another user pretty quickly. I've talked to them about it and gotten one of them into my Vivitrol program. It's helped her like it's helped me."

Frank smiled and waited. He knew Alan had more to say about the two new hires—local women with spotty employment histories. They had been hired because they were well-groomed and showed up to work on most days. Good help was hard to find anywhere, but especially in remote Defiance.

"My point is that somebody is pushing fentanyl and amphetamines on them. I can't tell who the pusher is yet, but the Jones woman is pretty far gone. Mabel Schmitz seems to be improving with the Vivitrol."

"What do you think we should do?"

We both know it's difficult to find good employees these days. You have resources I don't understand. I suggest you try to find who's pushing the drugs on them. The pusher doesn't seem like the usual street peddler. I think there's something bigger behind this pusher than you might guess."

Frank tried to hide his surprise. Alan Ackerman clearly knew more about his activities than he had realized. "I'm intrigued, Alan. Why do you say I have resources you don't understand?"

"I'm just guessing, Mr. Palermo, but I can't help but hear the talk when I serve dinner to your group. Your nephew and Mr. Browning obviously have considerable influence in banking and financial circles. I don't want to sound nosey. It's just obvious to me that your group has strengths that you don't advertise. The security you have around you is also obvious. I wouldn't want to mix it up with any of Mr. Browning's security guys. They scare me."

"They scare me too, Alan. I guess that's what they're supposed to do. I'll check with Mr. Browning and my nephew about your suspicions. We'll see what we can find out. In the meantime, keep up the good work around here. You've really turned yourself around."

"Thank you. I'm in a new study where they put the naltrexone pellets under the skin in my belly. The blocking effect lasts for many months. I don't have to go back for the Vivitrol treatment so often. That's saving me a lot of time. This time, I really think I can stay clean."

Frank set about finding the source for the fentanyl and amphetamine being fed to his two new employees. He asked Barney and Vinnie to involve their wives—Moselle because the employees liked her and confided in her and Rachel, a superb source to hack their phones and laptops. Moselle learned that the two recently hired women had been buying the drugs from a pusher across the river in Chesterfield. They met with the pusher weekly in the failing Chesterfield Mall to obtain their supply. The largely vacant mall was scheduled for demolition, a fate that seemed to be overtaking many old shopping malls. The land would be redeveloped into a high-end mixture of hotels, condominiums, retail shops, restaurants, and concert venues. In the meantime, the mall had become frequented by pushers, prostitutes, and homeless people. This particular pusher had opened a kiosk under the guise of vitamin, mineral, and herb sales. She was actually peddling dangerous drugs in a high-demand market—St Louis County. The problem for Frank was identifying where she was getting fentanyl, methamphetamine, and cocaine. That's where Rachel proved invaluable. She traced a convoluted trail of drugs from St. Louis back to New Orleans and originating in Mexico and Columbia. Associated with the drug traffic was a money trail that originated with shell companies tied to Sunshine Investment Bank in Road Town, British Virgin Islands.

The two newly hired workers were getting such a generous discount on the drugs that Frank suspected the entire operation had been designed to entrap them. His suspicion led

Rachel to further investigation that uncovered a wide-ranging conspiracy aimed directly at him and his restaurant. The drugs were being sold at a premium to other area residents. Frank figured this shadowy operation was not only aimed at damaging him and his restaurant, but it was also providing a tidy profit for the Sunshine Bank principals.

Chapter 6

As the summer of 2023 ended, the world maintained its weirdness. The war against Ukraine slogged along with Ukraine retaking occupied territory measured in meters a day. Missile attacks resulted in civilian deaths throughout eastern Ukraine, and sabotage of Russian installations became a daily event. Russia had pulled out of the deal to allow export of Ukrainian grain across the Black Sea. This forced shipment of grain by rail and trucks to adjacent countries. The railroad links were hindered by different track gauges between Ukraine and its neighbors, forcing unloading and reloading grain at the borders. Poor nations feared famine in the coming months. Vladimir Putin grew increasingly paranoid after Prigozhin's brief rebellion. His war plans awry, he sought weapons from North Korea's Kim Yung Un, the even more paranoid leader of the misnamed democratic people's republic. Smelling money, Kim took a 20-hour trip in his armored train to meet Putin near Vladivostok. Again, the trip was hindered by a difference in rail gauges between North Korea and Russia. This time, they changed the wheels on Kim's slow train at the border. After all, it was Kim's train, and he was staying in it.

In the United States, inflation continued, as anyone who shopped for food and gasoline could see. Thousands of immigrants who crossed the southern border were bused to large cities, straining social services and tempers. Political leaders bloviated or dodged the media entirely. Fear grew that the federal government might shut down in October due to lack of a funding resolution. Cancel culture raged, and the number of genders increased. And all this in a non-election year. Because of general dislike for the sitting president and his predecessor, people hesitated to think about 2024.

In the Midwest, Family and Home Bank, known to its founders as FAHB, expanded, stretching from the Dakotas down to Texas. Deposits increased, investments did well, and commercial and residential loans had low rates of default. "People are starting to notice us," Barney said to Vinnie at their weekly remote meeting in mid-September. "We're in the financial magazines and on cable news. I'll bet Treasury sends us another visitor any day now."

"I actually think it's time to stop growing. If we get much bigger, the regulators will be all over us. Right now, we're getting trashed on social media. Rachel thinks it's coming from the East Coast crowd and that turkey at Treasury."

"Kraken? That doesn't surprise me," Barney said. "That guy is unctuous ... downright slimy, but I'm not sure how smart he is. We need Frank to get involved with the bank. I've tried to get him to help us with investments, but he's dug in his heels ... he only talks to me in the pasture when my dogs are barking at the goats. I have a hard time hearing him, so I figure everybody else does, too. He *has* given me some good tips on investments when we're out there. He won't meet inside or put anything in writing. He and Helen are definitely going low-profile."

"I don't blame him. He's trying to abide by that consent order ... that's Uncle Frank for you. He's really a Boy Scout. He used that bank in Limassol for a good purpose, but he destroyed the bank ... destroyed the purpose and trust that goes into a bank. He knows it, and he's trying to atone for it in some way. I don't always understand him. He's too old-school for me. I love him and Aunt Helen both, and I want them to be happy. At least I'm glad you've got them sleeping up at your place on the bluff. They had no security down at the restaurant."

"The restaurant is still insecure. Anybody could walk in there and gun people down ... plant a bomb, and obliterate the place and everybody in it. It's a scary thought, but it's entirely possible. That restaurant is a big fat target."

"Rachel thinks that's exactly what they're planning to do. Val Constantin is their point man. He's delivering a bomb to the Jones woman ... you know they've got her hooked on dope. She plants the bomb in the basement, and they take out Frank and Helen and anybody else who's in there. They think they can make it look like a gas leak."

"Does Frank know about this?"

"Not yet. We're trying to learn more about their plans. With Harry Galanis and Davi Nara both dead ... I think they were poisoned ... this thing would only scare him more. We need to intercept the Jones woman before she plants the bomb. Rachel thinks it's going to happen at the end of September."

❧

Beulah Jones came crying to Alan Ackerman at the beginning of her shift on September 27. "I'm just so sorry, Mr. Ackerman. I know you depend on me. I'm in real trouble, and I don't know what to do."

Alan sat her down at the kitchen staging table. "I'm sorry, Beulah, I can see you're having a hard time. If it's about fenty, you know I can get you help with that. I've been through it too."

"It's about fenty and a lot of other stuff. It's killing me. I'm too up, and then I'm too down. There's no in-between for me. Now they want me to do something bad."

"Something bad, Beulah?"

Beulah drew a breath and wiped her eyes. "I know you know I'm strung out. You've been very kind to me. I really appreciate that. Now I don't know what to do."

Helen and Frank had warned Alan that Beulah Jones might try to bring a dangerous object into the restaurant. Alan was careful to conceal that knowledge. "Please tell me what somebody wants you to do."

"They want me to bring what they call a package in on Saturday ... put it in the basement by the gas line. I'm not very smart, but I'm pretty sure what they're trying to do."

"Do you think this package they're talking about might start a fire or explode?"

"That's what I'm afraid of. Oh, Alan, I know I'm a mess, but I don't want to get involved in something like this."

"Let me talk to Mr. Browning. You know he's experienced with things like this. Now you go on home today and rest up for tomorrow. Tuesday is our slowest day. We'll be okay without you for today. We'll get back to you about this in the morning when you come in. And please don't talk to anybody else, okay?"

Alan texted Barney and asked permission to come up to the blufftop compound. Barney surmised what was afoot and walked down to the restaurant to meet Alan. They sat at a table on the empty music patio. "I think she is being forced to bring a bomb into the restaurant," Alan said. "You know she's an opiate user. Whoever is feeding her the drugs thinks they can control her."

"I'm not surprised. It looks like their plans are firming up. Let her pick up whatever this package is, and we'll get it from her before she gets to the restaurant. Do you know when they plan to do this?"

"Next Saturday. They're doing a rehearsal on Thursday. They'll give her the drugs and the package on Saturday. It's our busiest day. If they set off a bomb during working hours, it could kill a lot of people."

❧

Margaret Benson called D. Oliver Reginald Kraken into her office at Treasury on Monday, September 29. "Reggie, I want you to go out to St. Louis again and talk to those Palermo people. We think their bank has gotten too large. Our risk assessment experts say they're overleveraged. We'll file the paperwork, but you need to put a little anxiety into them. If you succeed, they may make a mistake, and that could lead to a prosecution."

Kraken studied Margaret. He had tried to get more information about Margaret's prior interactions with the Palermo clan and Barney Browning, but he found no one at Treasury to answer his questions. Certain electronic files on the matter appear to have been erased. The East Coast organization had financed his education and placed him in the U.S. Treasury Department position when his academic career faltered. They seemed to consider him their government mole.

They only told him what to do, never why. Margaret told him what to do and why, but he never believed the why in her case. Her motivation was patently devious. The one common thing Margaret Benson and the East Coast organization seemed to share was an intense hatred for the Palermo family and Barney Browning. He jumped at the chance to get more involved.

"Sure, I'll go, Margaret, but I need help from you. The secretaries don't assist me with travel and communication. Will you tell them to arrange my trip out there? I'll need a car and a hotel room. I prefer the Ritz in Clayton."

"I'll ask them, Reggie. You know they're unionized. They have tight work rules. And you know your government stipend won't cover that hotel. You'll have to pay for that yourself. Before you go, we'll discuss a plan about what you'll say to them when you get there." Margaret didn't tell Reggie that his imperious manner was the obstacle to getting cooperation from everyone at Treasury. It was best to keep Kraken off balance.

After several bureaucratic delays, Reggie flew Southwest to St. Louis on October 7 and picked up a Cadillac Escalade XL at the airport. He had requested a first-class ticket on American, but Margaret Benson's secretaries thwarted him, maintaining that first-class airfare was against government regulations. Reggie knew Margaret sometimes flew first-class. He figured the secretaries hated him. The Escalade was more to his liking, although he had to pay for the upgrade himself. He could sit above the other drivers, and no driver would challenge him in the big SUV. His only problem was he did not know the way to Defiance, and he did not know how to use the GPS on his phone or on the vehicle. He asked for a paper map at the car rental lot, and the attendant gave him a puzzled look before handing him a map.

❧

Val landed at Spirit of St. Louis airport and passed through security without incident. His handlers had used his plane—a bitter irony. They had stopped at an airport in New Jersey to clear customs and immigration, then continued to St. Louis as a domestic flight. He picked up two new minders and the package at the airport parking lot. "I still don't know why you need me to do this," Val said.

"It's not about us ... it's about you." Said one of his new minders. "You need to do this to get your life back. We don't plan to talk about this again."

They drove a new Audi sedan to the Chesterfield Mall, where they met Beulah Jones in the largely empty east parking lot. During the short drive, they demonstrated the device with its attached remote detonator and GPS locator. Val had been given precise instructions for Beulah. As he took the package over to Beulah's car, he saw both minders recording him with their phones. He tried to smile as he handed her the shopping bag. "Here is the package," he said. I'm sure you know what to do with it."

Beulah placed the shopping bag on the passenger seat of her Toyota Corolla. "I have to put it next to the gas line in the basement ... with the logo on the bag facing the gas line. Yeah, I know what to do."

"Good luck. Don't hang around after you place the package." He then handed her a bag containing fentanyl tablets and powdered cocaine. Here's a little something extra for all your trouble." Val cast a casual glance at the nearby parked car containing Pauli Leone and his two gunsels before he walked back to the car with the two FSB minders.

"Done and done," he said as he settled into the passenger seat. He expected to be executed at that point by the man sitting behind him.

"Now we follow her to the restaurant," said one FSB man. "I want to see this event happen in person."

"Are you sure that's a good idea? I don't think we want to be around when that thing goes off." Val was happy to be breathing.

"Of course, it's a good idea. We want to see our device work. We have to record it for our superiors."

At that point, two of Barney's men, sitting in a distant car, disabled Val's new Audi with a strong electromagnetic pulse to its ignition system. Val's two minders immediately knew something was wrong. "This goddam car won't start. I push the button, and nothing happens."

Val sighed. He had expected a bullet in the back of his head, and he was happy to be talking. "Try it again. Sometimes, the ignition in these German cars can be tricky."

"It won't start. You understand what I say to you?"

The backseat man said, "Does the remote detonator work from here? What about the GPS?"

"The remote should function from 20 miles away. I don't know about the resolution of the GPS. The American satellites are getting old. We obtained the entire system in Transnistria, and it's probably old too."

"Maybe we should call a taxi ... how do you say it, a Uber?"

"You're crazy, man. If we do that, we might as well invite the police to join us. We can set off the device from here ... then call the airport. They'll send a car to pick us up. Now follow the device with your GPS tracker."

Barney met Beulah in the commuter parking lot at Highway 94 and I-64 across the Missouri River. She handed him the shopping bag but kept the drug bag hidden. Barney and one of his men donned gloves and examined the bomb. "Just as I thought," said Barney's man, a demolition expert. "It's a shaped composition device, probably British. The GPS tracker and the remote detonator look old."

At that point, Kraken entered the parking lot in his Escalade. Reggie got out and spread the paper map on the driver's seat. "Well, looky here," Barney said. "Guess who just showed up. Let's wrap this baby in the magnet sheath. We've got an opportunity here we can't afford to miss."

"This device won't take out the whole building," Barney's man said. "I think it's just designed to take out a wall and start a fire. The broken gas line will do the rest."

"It'll get the job done that I'm thinking about. Let's get going. Kraken seems to have figured out where he's at ... with a paper map no less."

Barney and his man followed Reggie along Highway 94 to the Relay. It was midafternoon, the lull between the lunch crowd and the evening rush. A warmup act featuring Louisiana Slim's Band was tuning up on the outdoor music stage, and Slim began to sing a zydeco song. Three spectators and a dog of uncertain parentage looked on. A warm October afternoon predicted a large crowd later in the music venue. Reggie arrived and backed his Escalade into a parking spot overlooking the bluff. He retrieved his briefcase, left his suit coat in the SUV, and marched resolutely into the restaurant. Reggie felt confident in his Turnbull and Asser vest, slacks, regimental tie, and Churchill cap-toe shoes.

Barney got out of his vehicle and clapped the bomb under the front assembly of the Escalade. He posted his man nearby to keep other people away from Reggie's vehicle. Then he drove the armored Navigator up to his blufftop home.

Helen sat in the Relay's dining room, watching cable news coverage of the horrific massacre of Israelis near the Gaza Strip. Frank was in the kitchen watching Lidia's Table on Public Television. Alan Ackerman sat at his computer, developing menus for the coming week. "See how she does it," Frank said. "She never uses a recipe ... just a little of this, enough of that. She makes you feel like you're a part of her family. She's a genius. I think she's got the best show on TV, period."

"That's what you think because she's the only show you watch," Alan said. "That's why it has to be the best."

Frank heard Reggie's distinctive voice as he began to harangue Helen in the dining room ... shouting at her about violation of banking rules and impending federal investigation. Frank hurried to the dining room. As he approached Kraken, a loud bang shook the building. The three of them rushed to a front window to see the Escalade flipping upside down and sliding down the bluff on its roof. A cloud of smoke and plastic parts rose from the Escalade. The vehicle burst into flames when it came to rest at the bottom of the embankment. Reggie muttered something incomprehensible.

"That your ride?" said Frank. It was a rhetorical question since the parking area was otherwise empty in mid-afternoon.

Reggie continued to be incapable of speech. "Looks like somebody blew it up," Helen said. "You'd better call a ride back to the airport. It's too far for you to walk."

Kraken found his voice and sputtered, "You don't understand. I left my coat in that vehicle. My billfold, my phone ... everything was in my coat."

"That's very unfortunate for you. I'm sure you have plenty of insurance. With your connections, you'll have no trouble persuading the adjusters." Helen paused and smiled at the stricken Reggie. "I tell you what ... I'll ask Mr. Browning if one of his men can drive you to the airport."

Chapter 7

Moselle and Barney stood at their front window watching two fire trucks pumping water on the burning Escalade. "Oh my God, Barney. I can't believe you did that." Moselle was furious after Barney explained the explosion and fire in the Relay's parking lot below them.

"It was impulsive; I admit it. I'm sorry about it, but the opportunity overcame me when I saw Kraken drive up."

"You really must control your impulses. I think the whole world has some kind of brain fog. We've lost control of our senses, every woman and man of us. I wonder if Covid has something to do with it. I recently heard a woman say she was a bilingual disabled, neurodivergent queer Black Latinx. I wrote it down and looked up the words. I'm still not sure what some of those words mean. I get the Black part, but the rest of it confuses me."

Barney was relieved Moselle had changed the subject. "I think it has something to do with the two sexes, sixty gender thing. I can't keep up with it, and I don't even try. I'm busting my backside, building a banking system in the Midwest. By the way, you need to be careful with your pronouns. People are easily offended these days by a simple him or her."

"Her or him, I don't care who I offend, my love. I'm past worrying about things like that. I'm trying to raise little Barney and keep you out of trouble. That's two full-time jobs right there." Moselle was still studying the smoldering Escalade when Barney jerked her sideways. A single bullet pierced the shatter-resistant window where she had been standing, burying itself into the opposite wall of the great room.

"They're shooting at us," Moselle said. "Do something!"

Barney was on his cell. "One round just came through the front window. Two up here for Moselle and the baby and two with me. He's straight across the road in that first clump of trees. I almost didn't see him." He pulled his XM7 and his handgun out of the hall closet. 'Please stay put, sweetheart. Two of the guys are coming to sit with you. The shooter is across the road. We're going after him. We've got to move fast. We'll talk when I get back."

Barney and his two men, all former special ops personnel, sped down the bluff in their two fortified ATVs. Unfortunately, by the time they crossed the road and entered the trees, the shooter had fled. They saw him in the distance, fleeing down a secondary road in a gray SUV with no license plate. He was beyond their reach. They searched the immediate area and finally found a shell casing.

Barney lifted the shell casing on a twig and studied it. "Looks like he was shooting an old Dragunov. I wonder what museum he stole it from. This thing dates to the Cold War."

"It's an antique, boss, but it gets the job done ... particularly at this range. Good thing you saw him in time. I'll check the serial numbers on the casing, and we'll see if we can lift some prints or DNA. We might get a lead on him that way."

"You two search the area and see if he left anything behind. I'll walk back. Now, I have to explain this to Moselle. I'd rather get a root canal than take the blame for this."

Barney put his guns away in the hall closet and faced a very angry Moselle in the great room. "Barnabas Browning! I can't believe what just happened. I was almost killed. I just can't believe it." Moselle had her hands on her hips, and her eyes were fiery slits.

"I'm sorry, baby. We didn't anticipate a shooter. We definitely dropped the ball on that one. We knew about the bomb but not the shooter. I'm going to put in better windows up here, and we'll increase drone surveillance. I'm already in the process of buying that property across the road, and we'll build another house there for our people. Nobody's going to drive us out this time. I'll see to that if I have to buy this part of the county."

Moselle glared at Barney in silent disbelief. Her eyes flashed fear and anger as she picked up their toddler and returned him to his nanny.

❦

Valentin Constantin found himself again in Road Town, BVI. His FSB keepers had returned him to Lettsome Airport in his own Gulfstream G550 and driven him to his rental home, where they deposited him without a word. Throughout the return flight, he complained that he had kept his end of the bargain to deliver the bomb to their operative in St. Louis, but they ignored him.

He had been two days in Road Town when the two FSB men entered his office on a Monday afternoon. "Good afternoon, Mr. Constantin," said the talkative one. "You have caused us some difficulty. We have decided to pursue a different direction with you. You will like our new plan."

"I did what we agreed on, whatever your name is," Val forced a smile at his tormentors. "I delivered the package. The rest of it was out of my control."

"Unfortunately, the original plan did not result in the desired outcome. This time, I think we have a better plan."

"What do you want me to do? Maybe strap on a suicide vest and walk into their dump of a restaurant? Is that what you want? I know you plan to kill me if one of your stupid plans ever works, so why don't we just get it over with right now. I'm fed up with your incompetence."

"Your sarcasm is not appreciated, and your anger is misplaced. You should direct your anger at the people who ruined your life. You can work with us, Mr. Constantin, or you can stay here and wait until your money runs out. We hear that possibility is imminent. We will certainly give you that choice. Now, please walk with us down to the quay, and we will tell you what we have planned."

The quay was almost empty in late November. A golden sun cast long shadows over the few fishing boats and pleasure craft that summer crowd, awaiting the influx of winter pleasure seekers fleeing the North American winter. Soft lapping sounds from the few boats and shrill cries from seagulls circling above punctuated the sunset's beauty. Val waited for his two handlers to catch up.

"Don't you find it a bit tiresome here this time of the year, Mr. Constantin? No parties, no pleasures ... really, no people." The short walk down to the quay had made the talkative one breathless.

"I don't mind it here if I have my freedom. Actually, I think Road Town is idyllic like this between seasons. Now, please tell me what you want from me."

"If you prefer us to be abrupt, we will oblige you. We want two things from you. We want you to work with Sunshine Investment Bank and we want you to reopen channels of communication with your bank in Moldova."

"I'm willing to work with the wretched bank on anything that is remotely legal. However, I have no traction with the bank in Moldova these days. I've been banished by the new management over there. Your colleagues took it over as soon as my brother Vladimir came to the America."

"We have arranged for you to have traction, as you say. We want you to begin buying preferred shares in a U.S. bank. It's known as Farm and Home Bank. It's in the midwestern part of the U.S."

"What money do you suggest I use? I have no funds at my disposal, and you know it."

"We will give you access to your assets here at the bank. We will also provide additional equity. You will be supervised."

"So, I'm buying stock in a bank somewhere in the desolate middle of America. There's nothing to stop you from doing that without me. Why don't you do this yourself?" Val sensed he was walking into another trap that he had no way to avoid.

"You advertise yourself as a banker, Mr. Constantin, but you are really no such thing. You are a promoter ... what the Americans call a rainmaker. We represent bankers and asset managers. Now, we intend to use your skills to make it rain for us."

Val looked at his handlers in wonder. "You gentlemen are beginning to amuse me. I don't even know your names, but your accent, Boris, or whatever your name is, puts you on the wrong side of the Urals. Siberia is a pretty desolate place, too. Now you're trying to talk American slang as if you know what you're doing. I hope your new plan is better than your old one." Val forced a smile and decided to pursue a more moderate direction. "Sunshine Bank is a short walk from here. I'll go there tomorrow if that's what you want. I don't see I have a choice."

"Not tomorrow. The bank is only open Wednesday to Saturday. We'll have our technical people waiting for you on Wednesday. You'll be making rain for us remotely. You will not regret working with us." Without another word, his two handlers turned and walked out of the office.

❦

Barney Browning thought his security system was adequate, but the sniper attack from across the road had unnerved him. He replaced the glass in their home with a composite transparent material that would stop multiple fifty-caliber rounds. He installed a better radar system and drone defense. He completed the purchase of the property across the road and began construction of a house there for two of his security team. The remaining weak link was the Relay restaurant. Frank and Helen insisted on working there every day. He saw no way to secure his friends in a building that was open to the public. He installed bullet-resistant composite in the windows of the Relay and positioned more surveillance cameras outside with a feed to his central surveillance system.

One brisk afternoon in late November, he drove his armored ATV down to the roadhouse. Alan served him a beer, and he joined Frank in the minuscule office that opened from the kitchen.

Frank was sipping a San Pelligrino. "How's it going, Barney? I'm glad to see you taking some time to relax. You might be working too hard. I see workmen all over the place around here. At least they keep us busy this during our slack time ordering food and drink."

Frank, the security around here is not good. Anybody could walk in here and pop you and Helen. None of your people are alert to what's going on around them. Please let me station one of my security guys in the dining room."

"You know he would stick out like a sore thumb. We can't run a restaurant like that. He'd be bad for business. Besides, he'd be occupying an income-generating chair."

"I figured that's what you'd say. Anyway, that's not what I want to talk to you about."

Frank waited. Barney had the look of a nervous banker. "What's up, Barney? You know I can't get involved with you financially."

"Frank, to me a bank is a means to effectively allocate capital. It's based on trust. You apparently saw it differently during the Suyu Bank debacle in Cyprus."

I admit I used that bank to defraud bad people. I was furious when the Russians invaded Ukraine. I used that bank to exploit the greed of those oligarchs. It was all about getting their money, and it turned out to be pretty easy."

"By doing what you did, you gave banks a bad name. Banks can only operate when there is trust among the parties. Otherwise, it can quickly become a scam."

"You're beating me up pretty good on this. I've also heard this lecture from Vinnie."

"You deserve it. You used a bank badly while you were trying to do some good."

"Guilty as charged. Now, please tell me what's really on your mind."

Barney sighed. "Our bank is under attack from several directions. Our stock is being bought up and shorted at the same time; our financial reputation is being trashed on social media, and the Treasury Department is hounding us."

"Well, if it's the same guy from Treasury with the funny name ... I think it's Kraken or something like that. You could blow up his house."

"Frank, this is not funny! The bank's in a bad situation. I need some help."

"You know I signed a consent order with the feds about financial involvement. I'll tell you three things ... otherwise, we're going to have to take a ride to discuss this privately. It's too cold right now to walk outside. First, I now have assets to help you with the stock buybacks. I'll start buying your stock. Second, Helen can help you with social media. She's a genius at that. Third, ignore the guy from Treasury ... Rachel says they call him Reggie at Treasury. It's an acronym; you can figure it out. He's in over his head." Frank smiled, "And I still think you should consider blowing up his house."

"We need to take a ride before this conversation goes any further." They walked out to Barney's armored ATV, an anomalous vehicle that looked like an obese golf cart. As Barney drove them up the bluff, he looked at Frank. "How does Rachel know about the guy?"

"I asked her to check him out. She thinks he may be in with the East Coast crowd. He lives in Chevy Chase. It's a small house ... no pets or people in there ... only him. Gas leaks happen all the time in Maryland, especially when people are at work."

"Forget it, Frank. We're not blowing up somebody's house."

"I don't see what the big problem is. You blew up his rental car."

"That was an impulsive act ... a mistake. I regret it. Moselle has been pealing skin off my back about it every day. I've rarely blown up private residences ... The few times I did, I had a good reason." Barney hesitated before he changed the subject. "Frank, you've got to understand me about this. We can't protect you and Helen down there at the restaurant all day. It's too public. Anyone can walk in there and start shooting. I need you to stay up at the house full time."

"Barney, I hear what you're saying. I'm trying to bring Alan along ... give him equity in the operation. I want him to take over. Hell, he could probably take over now." Frank thought about his next words. "What makes it hard for me is Helen really likes the Relay. The restaurant not only attracts the road crowd, the local folks have adopted it as their own. Helen's made some good friends here in less than a year ... probably more than she's ever had. The Relay has become a stage for her. The customers are her audience. She thrives on it. I'd hate to take that away from her."

"You've talked to her about it?"

"As much as anybody talks to Helen. She likes to live entirely in the moment and not think about the future or the past. Sometimes, I think she has trouble telling reality from theater. All the world is really a stage to her."

"I hope she understands she's not writing the script. Please try to get her out of there as fast as you can. Maybe Moselle and Rachel can talk to her. I'll keep my security guy upstairs. I'm also going to put another guy in the parking area. The world's becoming a very unfriendly place."

Chapter 8

The world continued its unfriendly ways in December. The war in Ukraine seemed to have settled into a stalemate. The Israelis resumed their offensive in Gaza after a pause to exchange Hamas prisoners for Israeli hostages. In an attempt at a trifecta, the socialist government of Venezuela announced it was annexing an oil-rich area in neighboring Guyana. The Venezuelan rulers had trashed their own lucrative oil economy. Why not steal an adjacent one? The Houthi rebels, who controlled a part of Yemen, continued to launch drones and cruise missiles at commercial ships in the Red Sea. The United States and United Kingdom warships kept shooting them down. What China would do about Taiwan remained the question of the moment.

The United States, supplying arms to Ukraine and Israel, seemed impotent to stop hostilities anywhere. If this was the case, why not arm Guyana? At least, it presented another opportunity to sell weapons.

In Defiance, the citizens settled into the holiday rush. Food being a staple of hospitality there, gifts of cakes, cookies, stollens, wine and beer inundated the staff of the Relay. On the afternoon of December 7, Barney, Frank, and Alan Ackerman sat at a table in the kitchen, planning the logistics of serving the influx of December customers and protecting Helen and Frank. Mozart's Third Violin Concerto played overhead. Frank thought Mozart helped him make decisions. The first movement helped him formulate information; the second movement helped calm his mind, and the third movement pushed him to the decision point. He could play the music he liked until Helen arrived at four p.m. When she arrived, contemporary country music ruled the sound system.

The adagio second movement was barely audible when a server set down a closed tin on the table beside them. "These just came from the church," she said. "The lady said she's a friend of Helen's. She said these are the best sugar cookies you'll ever taste."

"Before we start, I've got some news for you," Frank said. He pried open the lid. "These cookies are coated in confectioner's sugar. At least they'll be sweet."

"Don't eat those cookies! Put the lid back on!" Alan said. "There's fentanyl in there."

But he was too late. Frank and Barney slid from their chairs and collapsed on the floor. Neither of them had ever used opiates, particularly one as potent as fentanyl. They had no tolerance, and the fentanyl fumes from the tin were enough to make them pass out. Alan had protection with multiple naltrexone pellets implanted in his abdominal wall. He jumped up and replaced the lid on the tin. He was preparing to administer naloxone spray in their nostrils when a tall man walked through the open back door, holding a bottle of liquid and a fistful of cotton gauze.

Alan removed the lid and jammed the tin of cookies into the face of the approaching stranger. He held the tin against the struggling man's face until the stranger also sank to the floor. "Guess you must be at the end of your Vivitrol cycle, my friend," Alan said. "Let's see how you like your own poison."

He quickly sprayed the naloxone antidote into the nostrils of Barney and Frank and dragged them one at a time to the kitchen's open back door. They were both breathing and beginning to regain consciousness. He ran back for the tin and carried it outside to the trash dumpster behind the building.

Barney was sitting up when Alan returned. "What the hell happened?" Barney said. "That hit me so fast it had to be some kind of narcotic."

"I think it was fentanyl," Alan said. "If you haven't been exposed and you breathe enough of it, it can put you down real fast. Looks like Mr. Palermo's coming around a little slower."

"You saved our lives. I had no idea fentanyl could do that."

"It's killing more people than Covid, Mr. Browning."

"You okay, Frank? Alan thinks we got a dose of fentanyl."

"I went out like a light. Who's that back there lying on the kitchen floor?"

Barney began to collect his thoughts. "I think he was coming in here to finish the job. Alan, see if you can wake him up with the Narcan. I'd like to ask him a few questions. It's probably too late, but please walk out front and see if anybody's driving away. This guy's not a local. We might get a lead on who's behind this."

Barney called his security people and instructed them to take the awakening stranger to their new security building across the highway. He next called Moselle at their bluff house and told her to take little Barney to the safe room. He rose and extended a hand to help Frank. "How you doing, Frank? What's the news you had before this thing went down?"

The more vigorous third movement of the violin concerto was now playing. "I wanted to tell you that Patsy Salerno is coming up here. He says he wants to buy a piece of your bank. He seems quite serious about it ...and about the Narcan, we need to get it in the restaurant and everywhere else. We need it in our vehicles and in our pockets. Fentanyl can kill us quicker than men with guns."

❧

The meeting with Patsy Salerno took several days to arrange. Vinnie and Frank were opposed to it on general principles, but increasing financial stress on Farm and Home Bank made it necessary. Patsy wanted to meet at Vinnie's home on Lake Geneva in Wisconsin, but Rachel vetoed that idea. Vinnie suggested his office in downtown Chicago, but Patsy said the city was too dangerous. He suggested Barney's blufftop home. Moselle gave that idea a firm no. With the holiday rush, Frank could not close the restaurant for their sit-down. Too many patrons had already made reservations.

Barney and Vinnie wanted Helen to attend, but Patsy was firm about meeting only with the bank principals and no one else. Barney countered that Helen would sit in as an observer. She would not have a speaking part. After further wrangling, they finally agreed on Barney's new security building across the road from the Relay. Helen could sit in as a silent observer. There would be no recording or videotaping.

On December 13, Patsy arrived at the security building in a black Chrysler 300. The big sedan dwarfed the two all-terrain security vehicles in the small lot. He was accompanied by his bodyguard and an accountant. Barney, Vinnie and Helen met the South Florida contingent at the door and ushered them into a makeshift meeting room in the partially finished building. Utilities had been installed, and the room was warm. Alan and Frank had put out some snacks and bottled water before they returned to the Relay.

The five men took seats around the table after the Italians exchanged kisses and pleasantries. Helen sat slightly apart from them. Patsy took a sip of water and said, "Thank you for meeting with us. We appreciate how you've helped us in the past. We are especially grateful for the license of your warehousing and distribution software. It's saved us a great deal of money."

Patsy paused and studied Vinnie and Barney before continuing. "You understand why we're here. I sent you the proforma data on your bank. We know it's financially stressed. We can help with that."

Vinnie looked solemn. "It's stressed, Patsy, because you and your people in New York have been doing a hit job on the bank."

If you're talking about Vito and the stock purchases, I have nothing to do with that. Vito can't control your bank by purchasing non-voting shares. He doesn't understand about classes of stock. And besides that mistake … if people are shorting your stock, anybody with balls can do that." Patsy smirked in Helen's direction.

"Social media has been slamming us about everything the bank does," Barney said. "It's obviously a concerted effort."

"That's coming from the Treasury Department. Margaret Benson and her useful idiot, Kraken, are running that show. We have nothing to do with that. You gentlemen have made a formidable enemy in Margaret Benson."

Barney grew impatient. He had expected Patsy's opening gambit and wanted to hear the basic offer. "Mr. Salerno, with all due respect, what you are telling us is not news. I'm asking you to put your offer on the table."

"Our offer is simple. We want to buy ten percent of your bank, and we want to open a branch of your bank in the Miami area." Patsy paused and nodded to his accountant. "Of course, we'd have to see your books before any money changes hands."

Vinnie and Barney tried to hide their relief. They had expected a full takeover with attendant veiled threats of personal misery in the future. Patsy was sounding more like a South Florida businessman than a mob kingpin. "We can't give you the branch in Florida," Vinnie said. "We're a Midwestern bank, and we want to stay that way. We can talk about a ten percent equity position if the terms are right."

"What terms do you propose? You need money; we have it. It's as simple as that.'

"Nothing's simple with you, Patsy, you know that. We'll take it as a cash loan. Your equity position will depend on your future behavior. I'll have our lawyers in Chicago check with your people and draw up the deal." Vinnie cast a glance at Helen, who met his look and blinked once in return. "And the money can't come from your offshore bank. It has to come from a reputable bank here in the States. And you have to stop doing business with the Moldova bank."

"Agreed," Patsy said. "I'm not doing business with the Moldova bank. If anybody's doing that, it's Vito and his people."

"Another thing, Patsy. You need to call off Vito and Pauli. Pauli is a loose cannon."

"I'll try to work with Vito on that. I'm not sure anybody can control Pauli, but I'll try."

Your equity position with the bank will depend on your compliance with these terms."

Patsy managed to smile. "I'm surprised it worked out as easy as this. We'll head back to the airport. I'll have my people contact your lawyers. I'm happy we can work together." Patsy and his small entourage rose and gathered their papers.

"Would you like to come over to the Relay for some of Uncle Frank's food before you head back? His place has gotten very popular."

Patsy dismissed his bodyguard and accountant to the nearby craft brewery. Barney said he had another appointment. Helen politely demurred, saying she wanted to see her godchildren. Patsy, Vinnie, and Frank gathered around the restaurant's kitchen table. Alan served them linguine and clams accompanied by a dry Soave and busied himself with the dining room customers. Patsy stuffed his cloth napkin into the neck of his dress shirt and dug in. "This is pretty good," he said. "Maybe it could use a little more garlic, but it's just about perfect."

"It's my mother's recipe," Frank said. "Our customers seem to like it."

"I see the prosciutto."

"It's pancetta. We couldn't afford prosciutto when I was a kid."

"Something else is giving it a rich taste. I don't know what it is, but I like it."

"She always finished it with a little cream. That's the rich taste. We couldn't afford prosciutto. But we could always buy cream."

"Thank you. I see why your restaurant is so popular."

"You ready for Christmas, Patsy?"

"I don't do Christmas anymore."

Frank and Vinnie waited. Patsy's declaration about Christmas seemed unusual for an Italian. Patsy twirled linguine around his fork and took another mouthful. He pulled several clams out of their shells and twirled more pasta. He broke off a piece of bread and dredged it through the unctuous sauce, redolent in garlic and fresh herbs.

"We're still getting parsley out of the garden," Frank said. "Please try the salad. That's fresh arugula from the garden. Weather up here has been mild so far ... of course not as nice as you have in South Florida."

Patsy looked up from his plate and addressed Vinnie. "My wife passed away last October. Our two daughters are married and live on the West Coast. I don't see them or the grandchildren much with Magdalena gone."

"I didn't know about you losing your wife," Vinnie said. "Please accept my condolences."

"It was unexpected. We think she had a heart attack. She was a little overweight, but I never thought she would be the first to go. In my line of work, I always thought it would be me."

With that, Patsy removed his napkin from his shirt collar and pushed his chair back from the table. He looked at his empty plate and addressed Vinnie. "It's time for me to go. I'll call my people. Thanks for the meal. It was very good. Frank, I hope your restaurant continues to do well. I'll get my people in touch with you about the bank deal. I look forward to working with you. I'm sure we can work something out."

Patsy had his car meet him at the restaurant's back door. Frank and Vinnie saw him off and returned to the kitchen table, now cleared of their plates and two empty bottles of Soave. Frank called Helen and Barney, who joined them without delay. The kitchen was otherwise empty. Alan and his staff were on a break.

When they were all wedged around the kitchen table, Vinnie began, "Well, what do you think? I saw a human side of Patsy today I didn't know existed. He was genuinely mourning his dead wife and his distant family."

"Rachel knew his wife died," Helen said. "She didn't think it mattered to Patsy. I guess we were all wrong about that."

Barney looked at Helen. "What do you think about Vito and that skunk at Treasury? Do you think Patsy was on the level about that? And what about Constantin and the Kremlin?"

"I don't think he knows much about Constantin other than they're all still trying to wash their dirty money through the Moldova bank. Anyway, that's what Rachel's been telling me. I'm not sure he's coming clean about his relations with Vito and the New York families. I think they're all still working together."

"You're a better judge of character than most of us," Frank said. "What do you think about the Treasury guy, Kraken?"

"He seems to be on Vito's payroll and also getting a government paycheck. He gives new meaning to the term, double-dipping."

"The problem is we're getting all our information from Rachel and her hacking team," Frank said. "We need an independent source to verify some of this stuff."

Everyone looked at Barney.

"Whoa ... I think I know where you're going with this. I still have a few sources at the Pentagon, but if I start asking around, it could do more harm than good ... get more government people interested in us. You know what I mean?"

"Your contacts there won't know about much our East Coast colleagues," Vinnie said, "but I bet they'll know something about what the Kremlin is doing. I'm sure the Russians are our biggest risk right now. See if they know who's shooting at us and trying to poison us with fentanyl."

Chapter 9

January of 2024 featured more of the same. Wars in Ukraine and the Middle East continued. Inflation was said to be tamed, but people who bought food and gasoline didn't believe it. Urban crime was said to be decreasing, but people were afraid to go downtown. The southern U.S. border remained porous. Joe Biden looked increasingly frail. Donald Trump won the Iowa Republican primary on January 15, pleasing half the electorate and terrifying the other. The mullahs in Iran grew bolder. Pakistan and Iran bombed each other. Tinpot dictators the world over continued their acquisitive ways.

The acknowledged elite met to solve problems in Davos, Switzerland. The uninvited awaited their pronouncements about climate change, wealth redistribution, and the folly of war. The World Economic Forum had begun in Davos as a confab of top executives, bankers and financiers. It had become a media event—replete with celebrities, rock stars, thought leaders, influencers, change makers, early adopters, politicians, and others of that ilk. The little mountain town became so crowded during WEF week that high-end sex workers had to rent cabins and run shuttles to service their clients.

Vito Ragusa sat at his desk in his Long Island mansion, studying the weekly income totals for Family activities in the Five Boroughs. His two accountants sat across from him, waiting for his reaction to his declining fortunes. The numbers told an alarming story. Labor union activities and healthcare fraud were steady but not growing. Commercial real estate still had not recovered. Drug profits were lagging due to lethal competition and legalization by governments. Income from extortion, physical shakedowns and protection services appeared to be lost forever. His capos and soldiers feared to walk the streets. New York City had become too dangerous. His efforts to control a domestic bank had failed. His income from his offshore bank was not a topic to discuss with his accountants. That money rested in a different silo.

Vito put down his tablet and glared at his accountants. "These numbers are crap! How come our South Florida colleagues are making money, and we're going broke? Will you please explain that to me?"

We aren't sure, sir. We think Mr. Salerno and his associates are doing well with commercial real estate, construction, and waste management. Florida is growing … and it's a low tax state."

"I know about all that. Tell me something I don't know about. What's new with Pauli? He tried to kill anybody?"

"Pauli Lyon continues to conduct your business in Hartford and New Haven. As you know, you continue to subsidize him."

"Okay, okay, I get the message. I need to cut my overhead. I want recommendations from you about downsizing. We're going to have to let some street crews go, starting with Pauli and his crew. Nobody wants to work the streets anymore. If they don't make money, they got to go. I want a list."

"We anticipated that, sir. I'm sending you a link to activities of all your crews; it's arranged by collections annualized for the past three years."

Vito fumbled with his tablet and opened the link. He scrolled down the list and put down the tablet. "This is crazy. Half my crews aren't making money. The top half is carrying the bottom half."

"I'm sure some of it is related to the pandemic. Times were hard for all businesses."

"The pandemic is over. We can't go blaming everything on the pandemic. My guys on the street are coasting. These numbers show me I have to cut my payroll in half to turn a profit."

"As you can see, sir. The income trends are going up. We think it's a lag period after the pandemic. You might want to consider giving that part of your business a little more time."

"How much time you talking about? You guys always make me laugh. All you want to do is wait."

"We suggest another year, sir, before you make significant changes."

"I'll give them six months. I wait any longer, I'll be in the poor house. Now get me Pauli on the video call. Be sure it's secure. I want to see his face when he starts lying to me."

The accountants had also anticipated that request. They had Pauli waiting in his New Haven office. The link was established, and Pauli appeared on Vito's screen. "Hello, Mr. Ragusa; how you doing?" Pauli's face showed his perpetual smirk.

Vito was surprised that his accountants were doing his thinking for him. "Ah ... I'm doing just fine, Pauli. We're looking at the numbers down here, and what I'm wondering is what the hell it is *you* are doing. You're not making any money up there."

"The pandemic slowed us down; that's for sure, Mr. Ragusa. Now the weather's got us. We're covered in snow right now."

"I know about that, Pauli. I'm wondering if you're doing so much free-lancing, you don't have time for family business.

Now Pauli was surprised. "Really? I don't know what you're talking about, Mr. Ragusa. I'm doing what you tell me to do ... nothing more."

"Don't try to con me, Pauli. I know you were over in St. Louis when Val Constantin was there. One of my friends told me he saw you. How much did Val pay you? It don't look like you did him any good, whatever it was you did."

Pauli's smirk faded. "Ah ... that was just a one-time gig, sir. It didn't take us off our work around here very long at all. You got nothing to worry about with that."

Vito sighed. He knew his capos and crews free-lanced. Declining family business made it necessary. Everyone had to eat and make car payments. "The only thing I worry about, Pauli, is my bottom line. I expect you to take care of that and nothing else. We're going to have to make some changes around here, and you don't want to be one of them changes."

❧

Valentin Kostakovich Constantin sat in his office in Road Town, BVI, contemplating his own declining fortune. The harbor below him had filled with many pleasure boats from North America, here for the winter season—big sailing and motor yachts with all the accoutrements of ostentatious wealth, rocking gently at their berths. Even larger boats were anchored in the road, with an occasional dingy moving toward the quay.

January would have normally been Val's peak season, too—an opportunity to network and schmooze with the rich and famous. But his party invitations had decreased along with his fortune. The cache of money, jewels, and gold he had hidden in his rental villa was shrinking. It was being consumed by living expenses. He wasn't sleeping well, and he had lost 10 pounds in the last six months. Val now had to act as his own secretary. The only person remaining on his payroll was Alexis Smirnov, his fixer and procurer.

True to his routine, Alexis appeared at 10 o'clock sharp, immaculately dressed in a bespoke Seville Row suit and Churchill wingtips. "Good morning, sir, I hope you had a pleasant evening. What can I do to help you today?"

"Good morning to you, Alexis. Let us go over our current situation. First, can we review my financial picture? Are there any new developments with Sunshine Bank?"

"I'm afraid not, sir. Your money and securities are still basically impounded by the bank. We also received notification yesterday that they're reducing your monthly stipend in 2024."

"I expected that. What about my assets in Africa?"

"The proceeds from the sale of your diamonds are currently in a bank in Mauritius. Unfortunately, you cannot access it. The bank insists that you withdraw it in person. They're refusing to wire it without your appearance and signature."

"I mean my human assets."

"The members of the Wagner Group who worked for you remain unavailable. They insist that you still owe them money from their last contract."

"The Haitians are incompetent. We can't use them. That's out of the question. What about my plane?"

"As you know, your plane is under the control of Sunshine Bank. Recent flight logs and tracking data suggest the bank may be using it in the drug trade in South America."

"Thank you, Alexis. Would you mind waiting a short time in the outer office? I need to think about this situation ... formulate a plan as the Americans say."

Alexis bowed and withdrew to the outer office. Val studied the harbor and tried to imagine a way out of his dilemma. His assets were being depleted at an alarming rate. His bankers had become his captors. Two people who presumably represented the Kremlin were trying to hatch a plot to kill him. The only factor in his favor with the Kremlin twosome was their incompetence. He dismissed Alexis for the day. Val needed a plan, and he knew it had to be a good one.

Ten minutes after Alexis departed, his two antagonists appeared as if summoned by Val's disdain. "Good morning, Mr. Constantin," said the talkative one, the one Val thought of as Boris. "We are happy to bring you good news. We are ready to proceed with a plan against the Palermo people. We have identified our target. We will need your help."

They sat down facing Val before he had time to acknowledge their presence. In spite of his peril, these two were beginning to amuse him. "Another plan, eh? Tell me about it, please. I'd most like to hear about it."

"We will travel to their little town in Missouri. We will enter the restaurant and kill Frank Palermo. We have identified him as the source of our difficulties."

"So, you just walk in and shoot him, right? I'm surprised you haven't thought of that before. It would have saved your superiors a large amount of time and money."

"Your attempt at sarcasm and derision is misplaced. We are offering you freedom and return of your assets."

"That's what you offered the last time, and I haven't seen any of it. Your promises cannot be trusted."

"Perhaps our previous plans were too ... how do you say it ... sophisticated? This time, we have a direct plan that will succeed."

"And where do I fit in with this plan?"

"You have a valid U.S. passport. In fact, you have several passports. You will get us into the country and direct us to our target."

Val was surprised that these two had overlooked the fact that he, too, was a wanted man. "I'm surprised you boys haven't heard of Google Maps. That software will take you where you want to go."

"No, that is not what we mean. We have a need for you to accompany us. You will be the one who shows us where to find our target."

"What if I say no?"

"If you decline our invitation, you can stay here and lose the assets you have remaining. That is your choice." His two minders smiled at Val. "Perhaps you still don't understand," said the talkative one. "You will be the one who shoots Frank Palermo."

Margaret Benson studied her computer screen in the Treasury Department building in Washington. As Assistant Director of the Investigations Division, it was her job to identify banking problems before they occurred, or at least to identify problems early so that her division would not be blamed. She paid particular attention to Farm and Home Bank, a midwestern bank holding company that seemed to be growing in an alarming way. A recent sizable unsecured loan to the bank might open an investigative door for her. She decided to send Reggie Kraken back to St. Louis to investigate. Reggie was useful in a situation like this because he could irritate almost anyone. She called him into her office.

"Good morning, Reggie. Please bring me up to date on Farm and Home Bank."

"I think you know, Margaret. They received a big infusion of money from a dubious source. They're booking it as a loan. We're still trying to track down the details. It came through several intermediaries, but it looks like it originated from a little bank in West Palm Beach."

"How much was it?"

"It looks like about a hundred million dollars. The money moved through at least two different currencies, so our estimates are approximate. It saved the Midwest bank from going under. Their stock had cratered, and they had several big debts coming due."

"That's my estimate, too. How do you think a little bank like that could get so much liquidity?"

"I think you also know that answer. It looks like that little bank is connected to a much larger bank in the British Virgin Islands known as Sunshine Bank and Trust. The parent bank moved from Nassau to Road Town last year. The owners have regulatory and tax advantages in Road Town. I think the West Palm Beach bank is a sham. It's not doing much business, but it's got a U.S. charter."

"I think we are in agreement about the basics of this matter, Reggie. I want you to go out there again and meet with them. You can tell them we're opening a formal investigation centering on that so-called loan. I'll get the process going here. We're going to need high-level approval for this."

"I couldn't get any cooperation from the girls in the front office for travel and reimbursement the last time I went out there. I'm very busy, Margaret, and I don't like to arrange my own travel."

"I'll ask the ladies to assist you. This is a high-priority assignment. Success on your part will greatly assist your career advancement."

Reggie knew that Margaret had a conflict with the Palermo family in St. Louis and Chicago. The circumstances of the conflict were vague, and try as he might, poor Reggie could not ferret out the details. That lack of knowledge annoyed him. He wanted to bend Margaret to his will ... Or, even better, make her miserable and run her off.

Margaret knew Reggie had to pay for the rental Escalade that was destroyed on his last trip to St. Louis. The particulars of the incident remained unclear, but the burned-out hulk of the vehicle was a reality--on the internet and in several TikTok videos posted by anonymous government employees acquainted with Reggie.

After the Escalade went down the embankment in flames, Reggie discovered that he owned it. His car insurance denied his claim, making him personally liable for the replacement cost. The government never authorized such a luxury rental and refused to pay for its fiery destruction. Margaret and Reggie kept their knowledge of the other's failures unspoken. You never know when you will need leverage over a colleague in the government.

In this way, Reggie again made his way to St. Louis, but this time with a nonrefundable airline ticket, a strict daily stipend, and driving a rental Ford Focus—all courtesy of the U.S. government.

This trip was a big letdown for Reggie. It was his custom to travel first class. Government service was beginning to lose its attraction, no matter what his patrons in New York City told him.

Chapter 10

Frank hated January. The cold seemed to penetrate his bones—making him even more sluggish. Going to work every day became drudgery, but he had no alternative. Alan Ackerman wanted to buy the Relay. His only problem was lack of money and credit. Alan's previous performance with bank loans had not gone well.

Besides that, Helen had come to love their restaurant. It allowed her to perform in front of diners and music lovers. The Relay was her stage, and she wrote a new script every day. Frank saw her pleasure and loved her for it. That knowledge alone kept him going to work.

A bright February sun brought shirt-sleeve weather to Defiance. Frank met with the staff at noon to review plans for the monthly menus, purchasing and entertainment schedule. They sat on the covered outdoor sound stage on a day so warm the radiant heaters were unnecessary. Alan was present with his two assistants, plus the dining room supervisor, and the bookkeeper.

When they had finished the routine part of the agenda, Alan said, "Mr. Palermo, I have to tell you the naloxone is flying out of here like you wouldn't believe. We can't keep it in the dining room or the kitchen or on the sound stage."

"Who's taking it?" Frank knew it was a rhetorical question.

"I think it's the girls in front," said the dining room supervisor.

"It's people in the kitchen," Alan said. "Anybody walks through, they seem to know where it is. I can't keep it hidden."

"I'm not taking it," said the two sous chefs in unison.

"How much is that costing us?" said the bookkeeper.

"It's off the books; I'm getting it from the research program I'm in. Narcan's gone over the counter, but the pharmacies are price gouging on it."

"How much are you paying for it?" Frank said.

"I'm just getting it, that's all." Alan smiled. "The feds are giving the local program as much Narcan as they want. It's part of the research project."

"What you're saying is you're paying for it ... hell, we're all paying for it ... we're just doing it so indirectly we don't know it." Frank returned Alan's smile. "Anyway, keep it coming; maybe we can stop this part of the county from overdosing."

They finalized plans for February at the Relay. Warmer weather was coming, and with that would come larger crowds and the reopening of the music stage. Frank thanked his staff for their hard work. He drove his ATV across Highway 94 to meet with Barney and the security team. He knew that meeting would be more difficult because he would be a supplicant instead of a supervisor. Helen had begun sleeping above the restaurant many nights instead of going up to the more secure blufftop house. Frank refused to let her stay there alone, so he would drive down to join her. The security risk was frustrating Barney. They had one security person sleeping in another bedroom above the restaurant, but Barney feared that one man would be insufficient to stop a team of determined assailants, even with Helen armed to the teeth.

☙

Val Constantin's tormentors returned with specific plans to kill Frank Palermo. They walked into his Road Town office one morning in early February. Val dismissed Alexis and motioned them to chairs.

For the first time, the smaller man spoke. "We have our weapons hidden in a shed we're renting near that little town. We will take you out on our boat now and teach you how to shoot. Then we will all go to St. Louis, and you will shoot him. Do you understand?"

Val thought the clipped Russian accent placed the smaller one's origin near Moscow. He began to think of the man as Ivan. "Sounds like a plan to me. Who am I to ask questions? Let's go out to sea and start shooting." Val tried to appear cooperative. He was determined not to underestimate these two; they were naïve but formidable. He also had another plan in mind.

Out to sea they went. When Road Town had become a white smudge on the eastern horizon, Val's tormentors cut the engine and let the boat drift on a calm sea. The taller one opened a small case and said, "Take the revolver. Put it in your hands. We will show you how to load it and shoot it."

Val was surprised to see the Nagant revolver. "It's a Nagant. That's my favorite weapon. I'm surprised that you would choose this weapon."

"It's our job to know these things. Besides it being your preference, a revolver is more reliable. It's less likely to jam than a more modern weapon."

Val picked up the Nagant and shifted it from hand to hand. "It feels good. I think it's authentic. I assume you have some ammunition?"

"Here are three cartridges. I know you are familiar with the cost of these cartridges. I'm going to throw a large plastic bottle out into the water. May we see what you can do with this weapon?"

Val began to slip the three cartridges into the Nagant. His two minders produced their modern PL-15 handguns and raised them toward Val. "We see you are familiar with the Nagant. We expected that. We are pointing our weapons at you only as a precaution. We don't want you to get any bad ideas."

The Nagant was clumsy to load because it lacked a swing-out cylinder. When Val finally had the three cartridges in place, he raised the weapon and fired at the floating bottle, now about five meters away on the sea. Three holes appeared in the bottle at the waterline. The bottle began to fill with water and sink.

"Very good, Mr. Constantin," said the Muscovite. "You definitely know how to shoot a Nagant. You will have three cartridges to kill Frank Palermo. Then you will be free."

Val handed the pistol to the Muscovite. "I look forward to it, gentlemen. Now, may we proceed back to shore?"

They returned Val back to his office with instructions to wait for their next message ... when they would go from planning to action. Val thanked them and saw them out. He immediately called Alexis. When Alexis appeared, Val walked him out onto the quay. "Thank you for being available and prompt. I have a favor to ask of you. It will not be easy."

Alexis shrugged, and Val said, "I want to obtain an explosive vest. It must not be obvious. That means it must be very thin. I will also need a remote detonator device."

"Such a product will not be easy to find, sir. The manufacture of these vests, especially the sophisticated ones, is very restricted. It will take some time."

"I know that, Alexis. Please remember that money is a minor concern in this endeavor. Time is what we lack. I suggest you begin with your sources in Moscow and Tehran. I'm also willing to bet that a few groups in the Middle East have good products in this regard. My need is urgent. If you can find a suitable vest, you should have it sent here as quickly as possible."

❀

Barney walked into the Relay's kitchen in the late afternoon on the first Monday of February. The evening rush of diners had not yet arrived. Helen and Frank were sitting at the desk in Frank's tiny office, drinking a S. Pellegrino Limonata. Barney opened a satchel and pulled out two Kevlar vests. "I think you both should be wearing these vests while you're down here. They're level 3; that should stop a handgun round."

Helen and Frank responded with stunned silence. "Here, try them on," Barney said. "They're light. You'll hardly know you have them on."

Frank rose and donned his vest. "You're right. It is light. I can wear it under my kitchen whites."

Barney held out Helen's vest, and she shook her head in an emphatic no. "I can't wear this thing, Barney. It will make me look fat."

"You're kidding, Helen. We're talking about your life here."

"And I'm talking about my life too. I can't wear this thing. On top of that, it will block my access to my bra holster."

"So that's it," Barney said. "How many guns are you packing?"

"I have one in my waist holster. I keep it in the small of my back. I also have my micro compact Sig in my bra holster."

"Can you hit anything with that little Sig?"

"It's for close-in work. It's good out to about 20 feet. I think of it as my small room gun."

Barney looked at Frank. "God help us. I'm trying to protect you both. I'm supposed to be the security guy around here. More than ever, it looks like I should hire Helen to protect all of us."

"You got that right, brother," Frank said, "but I don't think you can afford her."

Helen rose and put her hands on her hips. She raised her shoulders and seemed to tower over the two much taller men. It was a familiar pose to Frank. Helen's anger was coming. "You both treat me like I'm a child. You hover around me and don't let me out of your sight. I'm sick of it! I can't live like this. I need to go shopping. We need to eat at restaurants. I need to go back and volunteer at Beaumont. I've had enough! I refuse to let anyone make me a prisoner. I want to act like a normal person."

Barney and Frank failed to respond. The thought of Helen as a normal person stunned them.

"And there is no way I'm wearing that stupid vest."

"Okay ... I hear what you're saying. I'll just leave the vest here, and you two can work it out. I'm not trying to start a fight." Barney beat a quick exit with Frank following him out.

They spoke in the parking lot. "I'm sorry about that, Frank. I didn't know I was going to set her off."

"Don't worry about it. The pressure's been building in her during the cold weather. What you're doing is right ... trying to protect us. I think she's got a bad case of cabin fever, and she's about to pop a cork. The only thing that will cure it is retail therapy. That's what Helen calls buying a bunch of stuff."

"If she goes shopping, we don't have a prayer of protecting her. I've tried to beef up security around here, fortified the restaurant, and revised the entrance road to make us harder to find. The thought of Helen out in public is a nightmare."

"I don't think we have a choice. Rachel has warned her that something's about to happen around here. I'm sure Helen knows what the risks are. She gets a little agitated when she gets frightened .. even more so when she gets angry."

"Rachel told Moselle and me the same thing. She thinks there's a hit team coming our way. If Helen goes out shopping now, she might as well paint a target on her back."

"I don't think we can stop her, brother. I'll bet she goes shopping tomorrow. Besides, Rachel told Helen it looks like I'm the one they're after. People in high places are still hopping mad about the money I sent to Ukraine."

"Well ... it was the oligarchs' money."

"Please ... let's don't plow this field again. We can argue about whose money it was until the sun goes down."

"I never said it was a bad idea. I just said it was risky. Vinnie and I always liked your motives. We've been sending some of our profits to Ukraine."

"You're sending money to Ukraine? I don't believe it! God help us. Now the bad guys will be after all of us."

"It looks like they already are."

∾

The interested parties journeyed To St. Louis in the following ways. Val and his two minders came in his jet. Val recognized his pilot from past days when the plane belonged to him alone. The bank had retained his pilot along with his plane for their drug trafficking. Val decided his old pilot would be helpful if his plan worked. Their party cleared customs and immigration at a small Alabama airport known for lax security. They then flew to Spirit of St. Louis Airport in Chesterfield, where they were met by another conspirator with their handguns. Before deplaning, Val solicited and received a business card from the pilot, who said he hoped they could work together again. Four large Russians in a black Lincoln trying to appear inconspicuous, that image did not auger well for anonymity.

Reggie flew a packed Southwest plane to Lambert Airport and picked up his rental Ford Focus. He made his way to Defiance with plans to browbeat his quarry. The four conspirators came with plans to kill people.

Reggie's trip was more interesting. He argued with the car rental people about the terms of his contract, whether he would refill his gas tank on return, and how to operate an uncooperative key fob. He missed his interstate connection and had to backtrack to get on Interstate 64. When he finally neared Defiance, he could not locate the turnoff to the restaurant. The entrance he remembered seemed to have changed. He pulled into a road with signs to the Relay that turned out to end at a large mound of fresh dirt. He had no directional software on his Ford. His phone software was no help; it insisted that he was on the road to the Relay. He finally abandoned technology and drove into Defiance to ask for directions.

Val and his colleagues drove slowly along the winding Route 94 to Defiance, some ten minutes behind Reggie. They had been careful about the speed limit, the need to use directional signals, and the requirement to look like they knew what they were about.

But they could not locate the Relay. As they backtracked along the road, they saw a Mercedes 300 sedan parked on the opposite shoulder ahead. A woman was standing beside the car, talking on her cell phone.

"That's her, I'm sure of it," said Val.

"Who?" said the talkative one.

"Helen Palermo. I'm sure that's her. This is a stroke of good luck. I can't believe it. Stop and let me talk to her."

"We cannot deviate from the plan. If she sees us, we will have to eliminate her. She can identify us."

"Nonsense! Pull over in front of her. We can take her with us. She will be valuable to us as a negotiating tool. She can be very useful. There's no need to kill her when she can be of use to us."

They pulled across the road and parked to block the front of Helen's vehicle. Val got out and approached Helen. "Mrs. Palermo, may we help you? It looks like your vehicle is disabled. We can at least give you a ride."

"There's nothing wrong with my car that a can of gas won't help. Who the devil are you?"

"I'm Valentin Constantin. I've done business with your husband. I think we might have met on at least one occasion."

Helen began to back away when Val lunged at her. Before he reached her, Helen took his photo and threw her phone deep into the roadside bushes. Another man bolted out of the car, and together, the two men wrestled her to the ground. Rough groping hands quickly found her gun belt. They ripped it off and manhandled her into the trunk of the Lincoln.

"We need to find that phone," said Valentin Constantin.

"Forget it. We can't stay out in the open like this. She threw it so far into the woods nobody will ever find it. We must go now."

Chapter 11

Helen had briefly lost consciousness during the roadside assault. When consciousness returned, she became aware of men yelling at each other inside the car. She heard three, maybe four voices. They spoke alternately in English and what she thought was Russian. They sounded confused about the location of the Relay, which seemed to be their destination. Barney had done a good job of changing the entrance and the signage. She heard her captors decide to drive into town and deposit her in what they called the shed. She probed herself in the dark trunk. All body parts were moveable but sore; apparently, no bones were broken. Her Ferragamo jacket and Ravella blouse were ripped and dirty. Someone would pay for that. They had taken her gun belt, but they had missed the little gun in her bra holster. That gun would give her an edge. She only needed the appropriate time.

When the car stopped, she feigned unconsciousness. She felt rather than saw daylight when the trunk opened. Rough hands yanked her from the trunk and dragged her limp body into a dwelling.

"You think she's dead?" That was the voice of the one who called himself Valentin.

"There is no possibility she can be dead. I did not strike her that hard. Perhaps she struck her head when you put her into the boot." That voice sounded foreign. She had never heard that voice before.

The men propped her into a straight-back chair and zip-tied her feet and wrists.

Helen began to utter a soft, groaning sound. She opened her eyes and stared at the nearest man, the one called Val, who gave her a salacious grin. Helen found him revolting—a combination of sophistication and menace.

Her thoughts were beginning to coalesce. The one called Val would be Valentin Constantin, the Moldovan banker Frank had colluded with on the money laundering scheme. "Who are you people? What do you want? I've never seen you before." Helen began to sob, assumed a look of terror, and made her body shake.

"You should be frightened. You would be even more afraid if you knew what we are preparing for you and your husband. Now shut your mouth, you *cyka blyat*!" One man slapped her face hard and put duct tape over her mouth. Another man put a cloth bag over her head.

"Enough of this!" said Valentin Constantin. "We came here to do a task. Let us do it. We can return to the woman when it's done. We may still need her."

"I say we dispose of her now." The fourth voice was cold, measured. Helen heard danger in that voice. "The first thing we do is we find their restaurant. They've changed the entrance. Even our new GPS software doesn't work. Maxim, you have the best speaking voice. Please will you walk over to that bar across the road and ask directions to the Relay restaurant?"

Helen heard the man known as Maxim walk out the door. Now, only three men remained. She could make out their silhouettes through the cloth bag. Two of them were busy checking their handguns. The one known as Val paced about the small room, occasionally looking out the window. Helen thought the odds were improving, but they still did not favor her. She guessed they meant to wreak havoc at the Relay. If they did not kill her now, one of them would have to stay to guard her. That would be her time to strike. She tried and failed to make out the license number of her abductors' vehicle through the window. It was too far away, and the window was dirty. She waited and counted her breathing. She must remain calm.

Maxim returned. "The *krestyanin* over there says the entrance road has changed. It's unmarked, but everyone around here knows where it is. He said it's the unmarked road beyond the road with the sign for the restaurant." Maxim paused, "They're all drunk in there. They looked at me strangely."

"We go now. We will find this restaurant. This should not take long. Maxim, you will stay here and guard the woman. Kill her if she tries to escape."

☙

By this time, Barney and two of his men had found Helen's car. Barney quickly surveyed the area and sent his men into the roadside bushes. One of them soon came back with Helen's phone. For once, Barney's planning had worked. Helen had done what he had prearranged with her. She threw her phone precisely perpendicular to her car—in a direction where they would know to search. He fumbled with her phone and called Frank's cell phone. "Frank, it looks like she's been abducted. All her purchases are still in the back seat of her car. I don't think this was a robbery. She had enough stuff from Saks and Neiman in the back to make a thief salivate. I think she got a photo of one of the bad guys. I'm sending it to you."

The photo appeared on Frank's phone. "That's Valentin Constantin. I'm sure of it. That scumbag kidnapped her. Wait a minute; I'm getting another call on my cell. It might be about Helen. I've got to take it. I'll call you right back."

Frank returned Barney's call within a minute. "Barney, they just called me from the brewery in town. They say two different guys came in there asking directions to the

Relay. They didn't look like locals. Nobody in the brewery recognized them. One of them talked like he was from way out of town ... with a foreign accent. You know what I mean?"

That sounds like trouble coming your way, Frank. I'll send my men to help you. I'll go look for Helen."

"Don't worry about me. Take all your guys and find Helen. I'll call the county cops. They'll be here in no time flat. What we need to do now is find Helen ... and quick. She's in serious danger."

Frank called the St. Charles County police and requested immediate assistance. He told the dispatcher that he had a situation with armed men nearby. The dispatcher interpreted this message to represent a hostage situation and sent two squad cars and a negotiator to the entrance of the relay, which, of course, represented the dead-end road with entrance signage for the Relay. They drove back to the entrance sign and called their dispatcher to request further instructions.

Frank stood at the Relay's front door and watched his lone security guy jump in his car and race off to join Barney's crew. Soon after, the Lincoln sedan pulled into the parking lot, and three men approached the door. Frank recognized Valentin Constantin and retreated into the restaurant.

Midafternoon was always a slow time at the Relay, especially in the cooler months. Frank shooed the few diners through the kitchen and out the back door. Alan Ackerman insisted on staying, but Frank ordered everyone in the kitchen to run out the back door. He assumed that this crew of villains had already killed Helen. He was now prepared to die with her. He turned to face the three men as they entered the dining room.

Val took the lead. He marched toward Frank and stopped about six feet away. He pointed the little revolver at Frank's chest. The two men who flanked him had their weapons drawn and pointed at the floor. "Mr. Palermo, I never liked you. You have caused us untold trouble and loss of our assets. Now you will pay for what you have done to us."

The Nagant discharged a round, hitting Frank squarely in his chest. The impact knocked him back, overturning a table and two chairs. Frank lay sprawled on the floor. Val immediately turned and shot each of his minders in their open mouths. Both men dropped dead where they stood. Val put the Nagant in his right coat pocket, put one PL15 in the other coat pocket, and the other in his belt. He pulled the key fob from a coat pocket of one dead man. He saw Frank motionless on the floor and walked out the front door. This encounter had gone according to his plan. Now he must find a way to get to Africa.

He strode into the parking lot as Reggie drove up. Serendipity favored Val once again. He hailed the driver and indicated that he should lower his driver-side window. Reggie complied and Val pointed the PL-15 in Reggie's face. "I need a ride to the airport," he said. "You look like the person to take me."

"But I just got here. I have business with the owners. I'm from the Treasury Department in D.C."

"Good for you … now you're just about to leave. I have a plane waiting for me, and I don't want to be late."

As they exited the parking lot, Val detonated the explosive vest that he had removed and left in the Lincoln sedan. The explosion flipped the vehicle over and then down the embankment. The sound and light show of dust, flames, and smoke was visible to Val and Reggie.

"That was entirely satisfactory," said Val.

"It looks remarkably like something I've seen before," said Reggie.

Upon entering Route 94, they saw the two St. Louis County police cruisers parked at the old entrance to the Relay, their lights flashing. "Apparently, even the police cannot find that accursed restaurant. I'm going to Spirit of St. Louis Airport. Don't exceed the speed limit."

"I don't know the way. This is outrageous what you're doing to me. I protest. Don't you know kidnapping is a federal offense?"

"Merely head back to St. Louis. I'll show you the way. It will also give me time to get to know you. You sound like an interesting fellow."

Helen sat quietly sobbing, her head down and her body trembling. The room was warm, but she was adept at shivering. She was aware that her captor sat nearby. She could smell him.

"You know something, Helen, that's your name, am I correct? You are very attractive for your advanced age."

"If you take the bag off my head, I can see you. Now you are only a voice to me. Let us converse face to face."

"I know you are a dangerous woman. If I remove the bag, you must promise me to cooperate. I do not want to shoot you."

"I'm not that dangerous. I am just a poor helpless woman, held captive by a man I do not know, and I cannot see."

"I will remove the bag. Do not move. I am pointing my gun at you."

Helen recognized the peculiar odor as a combination of garlic and cologne. "Thank you, I appreciate that. Now I can see you. Oh, you're handsome." Helen gave him a radiant smile. "May I ask your name?"

"I prefer not to tell you. I may have to shoot you later. But if I don't have to shoot you, then you will know who I am."

Helen thought garlic and cheap cologne would be sufficient to identify this boy, but she smiled and soldiered on. "Please let us not talk about shooting people. We are here together. We are alone, trying to get to know each other. Isn't that enough?"

"You are pretty, too. I am sorry they hurt you and tore your clothing."

"Don't you find it hot in here? I feel like I'm on fire. I really need to cool off. Please untie my hands so I can fan myself."

Maxim complied. He cut the zip-tie with his Swiss army knife, all the time keeping his PL-15 trained on her.

Helen massaged her wrists and unbuttoned the top of her blouse, exposing a hint of cleavage. Her captor continued to stare at her breasts.

"I hope you don't mind me saying this: I am not very good with English. You have a beautiful face ... and beautiful breasts also to be such an old lady."

"Thank you for the first part. If you put the gun down and come over here, I will show you more. You can touch what you've been looking at so intently." Helen hoped she had not oversold her invitation.

Maxim stood, and Helen said, "Please put the gun down. You will need both of your hands to do this."

He put the PL-15 on his chair and walked toward Helen. She opened another button with one hand and jammed the other hand down her blouse. In one motion, she pulled the little Sig from her bra holster, released the safety and shot him in each shoulder. The gunfire made her ears ring.

Maxim fell to the floor in agony. "Goddam you, you shot me. I was trying to be nice to you, and you shot me. Now I'm going to bleed to death."

Helen holstered her gun. She stood and lifted the front chair legs out of the ankle zip-ties. She walked over to Maxim's chair and retrieved his PL-15. "There, there, it's not so bad. I aimed high to avoid the artery. We'll get some pressure on your wounds. Do you have a phone?"

Maxim had no phone. His organization never sent a junior operative on such a mission with any sort of identification. They were only furnished with weapons.

Helen looked out the window and saw Barney, Frank and several of their security people coming toward the little building. She opened the door, and they rushed in. Frank brought up the rear. "Sweetheart, you're alive," he said as he embraced Helen. "I'm so glad to see you. I was afraid they had done something terrible to you."

"This boy had something terrible in mind, but he was unable to turn it into action. Please get him some help. He's bleeding profusely."

Helen studied Frank. "You winced when you hugged me, and you're moving slowly. What did they do to you?"

"Constantin tried to kill me. The Kevlar saved me, but I'm going to be sore for a week."

"That's another score we'll have to settle, darling."

They called 911, and Barney applied his considerable first-aid skills. Maxim would likely survive, but he would have to find a new line of work. He would make a very poor assassin, given the function of his upper extremities.

Chapter 12

Val stayed busy with his phone as Reggie exited Route 94 and merged onto I-64 toward St. Louis and Spirit Airport. He called Alexis and told him to get ready for a quick departure. They were leaving Road Town for good. Getting ready in this context meant retrieving all his personal wealth hidden in the rented villa and meeting the plane at Lettsome Airport in six hours. He then called his reacquired pilot and told him to prepare the plane for an overseas flight—a plane that again belonged to Val alone. They would be returning to Lettsome Airport, but only to pick up Alexis Smirnoff and some baggage. The pilot must work out the route to Africa. They would fly to Lagos and then on to Nairobi.

Val put down his phone. "There," he said. "That's done. We're on our way. What's your name? For some reason, I think I know you."

"I'm D. Oliver Reginald Kraken. I work for the Treasury Department in Washington, D.C. I don't think I know you, sir."

"I think you work for someone else. I think you work for people associated with Sunshine Bank. That means you have a close connection with a particular criminal element."

"That's preposterous. I work for the U.S. government and no one else. You are sorely mistaken."

"No ... I think I'm correct in my assessment. I've seen your name on payroll statements from the bank in question. My people are very good at ferreting out private information. I'm certain I know more about you than you know about me."

"So, what if I do work for someone else? I don't know what that may have to do with you. You seem to be a fugitive to me. You're trying to get out of the country. I want nothing to do with you, sir."

"Au contraire, you have everything to do with me. You can choose to die at the airport here, or you can accompany me to Africa. I think you will be very useful to the organization that I'm building over there. I obviously can't leave you here alive. You would sully my reputation,"

Val, Alexis and Reggie flew to Africa, ferried by Val's reclaimed pilot and accompanied by many U.S. dollars, gold bars, loose diamonds and multiple guns—all of which would prove useful on a continent where Val had many friends and connections ... and quite a few enemies. Val was preparing to create a new life and persona for himself. Africa offered him the possibility of wealth and power, but most important, it offered freedom. The diamond trade, vast energy resources, and security services for numerous African politicians beckoned. He planned to establish an operations base in central Africa, perhaps the Central African Republic. His base of operations was unimportant; he was certain that many countries over there would welcome him. At least their political leaders would welcome him. He would reorganize the remaining Wagner group operatives that had not been ordered back to Russia. The future appeared bright, almost unlimited.

⁊

Helen, Frank, Rachel, Vinnie, Moselle, and Barney gathered at the Relay for a celebratory dinner on the first Monday in March. Alan Ackerman and his wife, Betsy, laid out a spread for them—grilled butterflied leg of lamb, roasted vegetables, pasta shells with asparagus pesto, and fresh Italian bread. Dessert was mixed berries over homemade sugared mascarpone. Frank supplied two bottles of a 2010 Barolo that Barney had been properly cellaring for him. The wine had only now entered its drinking window.

They were a close-knit group now. Rachel with forensic accounting training, but also superior hacking skills. She had been a math major in college who liked puzzles and riddles. She first took up computer hacking as a hobby. She was soon on the dark web and connecting with professional hackers all over the world. Her talent was quickly evident, helping her gain access to their networks. After her marriage to Vinnie, she had the money to pay for premium hacking services. Rachel was a young mother only on the surface of her life.

Moselle had a career as a military policewoman with a background in theater. She had starred in high school and college productions—a top cop and a talented actor. She was definitely someone not to be underestimated. When she and Barney married, she retired and pursued a different career path—managing his investments. Another young mother only on the surface of her life

They toasted with the wine and dug into the food. "Thank you all for coming to dinner," Frank said. "We've decided to close the Relay on Mondays. The staff needs a rest since we've gotten so busy. Once we get through the summer rush, we may close on Sundays, too."

Helen smiled at Frank. "Darling, closing the Relay for a day or two a week is only a partial solution. The restaurant will still be a strain for you. You walk like someone hit you with a brick. You really need to slow down."

"Somebody did hit me with a brick, and I've already slowed down as you can see. You've also seen the bruise on my chest. I wouldn't be here if I hadn't been wearing that Kevlar vest under my whites. I'm hobbling now, but I'm getting better every day. I'm a lucky man. It's you I worry about, my dear. Those goons put you through hell. I hope and pray you won't leave me this time."

"Don't worry, darling. I plan to stick around. I love the Relay. And it needs me. Our patrons want to see me as much as they like to come here to eat and drink. I've come to love Defiance, too. I like the people around here."

"Those villains paid for it," Barney said. "Two of them dead and the third with both shoulders reconstructed."

"What are the county cops saying about the shooters? Vinnie said. "I'll bet they haven't seen anything like that in a long time around here."

"They're accustomed to gunfights in St. Charles County," Barney said. "The drug trade guarantees that. It's the shooters that surprised them. Exotic guys from Russia shooting it out in Defiance was a novelty. The FBI and other government agencies quickly became involved in the investigation. They say the two recently deceased shooters worked for the GRU; it's a security branch of the Russian military. Everybody's afraid of that outfit. Ballistics indicate that the rounds that took out the two GRU guys came from a Russian gun. It's all on our surveillance cameras. Constantin shot them at close range with a very old revolver, an 1895 Nagant. Those two Russians were wanted big time by Interpol and national police in Poland and Slovakia. They had a rap sheet as long as my arm. They say the guy with the shot-up shoulders was a new recruit. The Russians are hurting for personnel in everything they do."

"Too bad one Russian got away," Rachel said. "And a very dangerous one at that. Valentin Constantin will bring trouble with him wherever he goes."

"it's beginning to look like another bad boy got away. Patsy tells me he thinks Kraken went to Africa with Constantin. We don't know whether he was willing or if it was at gunpoint. The Treasury Department isn't talking about him. Vito is being very quiet about his whereabouts. I wonder how long it will take Kraken to wear out his welcome over there." Vinnie seemed uncertain about Kraken. Rachel knew a way to locate Kraken but she maintained her silence.

The diners concentrated on their meal. Rachel always knew more about people than she divulged--an unpretentious everyday new mother with a secret electronic hacking team of freelancers that extended from Eastern Europe to Southeast Asia. Her motherhood was obvious in the person of her beautiful little girl. Only her family and a few close friends knew about the second part. This occasion was the rare time when she talked freely because she felt comfortable with her family and friends. "Constantin has amassed wealth and power, but he's having trouble establishing a base. I think he wants to locate his operation in the middle of Africa. It turns out he's not as welcome there as he thought. His reputation preceded him. He's got that big jet to take him anywhere ... that is, anywhere they don't try to arrest him. He may have to set up shop on Mauritius or an even smaller island off the eastern coast. It probably doesn't matter. His clients will come to him wherever he is. He's got the resources and connections. He's pulling together the Wagner group in Africa ... at least what's left of those guys. Putin sent most of them back to the front in his war in Ukraine. I think we'll hear from Constantin again. He's not going away. He likes the spotlight too much."

"Let's don't spoil a good meal talking about that despicable man. He may think he has a score to settle with us. As far as I'm concerned, we have a bigger score to settle with him. If he comes around here, I'll shoot first and answer questions later." Helen's eyes displayed a determination that was belied by her sweet smile.

"What's up with your parking lot, Uncle Frank? I saw you're putting up a fence around the embankment."

"The police made us do it. They said too many cars are catching on fire and rolling down the embankment. We're also putting in a small shrub and herb garden where the two cars blew up. Ironic that it happened in the same parking space. The hole's already dug. The explosions did the heavy work. All we had to do was fill it with topsoil. We're going to call it the memorial garden of exploding automobiles. That name is unofficial ... known only by our little group, but I'm sure the word will get out. It's one secret we don't have to keep."

"Are you two ever going to slow down?" Moselle asked. "You seem to be planning for the long term with the Relay."

"We're selling the restaurant operation to Alan," Helen said. "We'll carry the loan, and we'll continue to live upstairs for the time being. "Alan wants me to keep working part-time in the dining area. We have some plans for collaborating with the nearby wineries to feature some of their wines in the concert area ... maybe a wine bar with rotating selections. Frank has some firm opinions about Missouri wine. He's also thinking about building a house for us around here. This area is where we want to live. I don't ever want to leave, Of course, Farm and Home Bank can carry the loan for Alan if you're interested. Your bank seems to be buying real estate all over the Midwest."

Moselle laughed and gave Helen a high-five. "You answered my question. I can't wait to see what happens around here with you two as permanent residents."

Barney joined in, sounding more like a staid banker than a former commando. "Farm and Home Bank is growing beyond our wildest dreams. In my opinion, the banking crisis isn't over. A great many mid-sized banks in the Midwest are distressed. We could buy several more right now, but we don't want to attract too much attention from regulators. That's one reason why we aren't planning to get into real estate deals like the Relay. Right now, we're concentrating on buying commercial buildings that we can remodel as the market dictates ... that and putting up new modular construction that we can convert as needed. Now, don't get me wrong about Alan. I love the man; he saved my life, but he's not a good loan risk. No small restaurant is a good loan risk. We'll let Helen and Frank cover Alan's deal. They're back in the money again."

About the author

First, I am not a chatbot. I am a conscious person with neurons that think and fingers that write. But I have been trained. I live to read. I was an English major in college while I picked up enough science and math credits to go to medical school. My favorite authors are Jane Austen for narrative and Elmore Leonard for dialogue. I also recommend Mikael Bulgakov's brilliant novel, *The Master and Margarita*. I like music, food, wine, and cooking. I try to garden but rabbits usually beat me to the produce. I cherish my wife and family. I go to church on Sunday and work every day. Like Frank in these stories, my life is quotidian except for the occasional flying leap. These stories aim to show life from the perspective of an older couple. Like the rest of us, Helen and Frank are trying to survive, maybe even thrive.

-Thomas Morgan

www.ingramcontent.com/pod-product-compliance
Lightning Source LLC
Chambersburg PA
CBHW070402200726
48294CB00003B/1047